ADVANCE PRAISE

"Sly, knowing, and hilarious, *Heart Attack and Vine* is a perfect caper book set inside Hollywood's Dream Factory that just screams 'movie!' Studios, please option this immediately. With its nonstop action, snappy dialogue, and wisecracking characters, this send-up of Hollywood is a surefire winner."
— **Denise Hamilton**, bestselling crime novelist and editor of the Edgar-winning anthology *Los Angeles Noir*

"Like Kurt Vonnegut and T. Jefferson Parker teamed up to write a mystery."
— **W.L. Ripley**, author of the Wyatt Storme mysteries

"Crush is back in town, and the Hollywood sign is in wicked, Technicolor flames. Phoef Sutton's rabid charmers break hearts and redden all carpets, and his pages fly by on winds of wit. This sly writing has Chandler cross-hairs and is pure, CGI-free magic."
— **Richard Christian Matheson**, Amazon #1 bestselling author of *Dystopia* and *Hell Comes to Hollywood*

"Insanely fun and readable. Sutton writes like a great raconteur tells a story."
— **Hart Hanson**, writer/creator of *Bones*

PRAISE FOR *CRUSH*

A *Kirkus* 2015 Best Mystery/Thriller

"As slick as a switchblade with a pearl handle."
— **Lee Child,** *New York Times*–bestselling author
of the Jack Reacher novels

"With nonstop action and variations on the man-with-a-gun distraction that go Chandler one better, *Crush* is also an homage of sorts to Chandler's pulp fiction and, moreover, Elmore Leonard's crime fiction. Like Leonard, Sutton writes great dialogue and lavishes almost as much care and attention on his villains as he does his heroes."
— *Los Angeles Times*

"This one could make it to the big screen, but don't wait for the movie. Buy the book. It may be the first of a long series."
— *Kirkus Reviews*

"Tailor-made for the big screen."
— *Publishers Weekly*

"A swagger of a book whose ironic tone reveals the author's past... Literate dialogue among the karate kicks and snapped forearms makes this an easy sell to anyone seeking a sassy diversion."
— *Booklist*

HEART ATTACK AND VINE

A CRUSH NOVEL

PHOEF SUTTON

PROSPECT
·PARK·
BOOKS

Published by Prospect Park Books
2359 Lincoln Avenue
Altadena, California 91001
www.prospectparkbooks.com

PROSPECT
· PARK·
BOOKS

Distributed by Consortium Book Sales & Distribution
www.cbsd.com

Library of Congress Cataloging-in-Publication Data

Names: Sutton, Phoef, author.
Title: Heart attack and vine : a Crush novel / by Phoef Sutton.
Description: Altadena : Prospect Park Books, [2016]
Identifiers: LCCN 2016020626| ISBN 9781938849848 (hardback) | ISBN 9781938849688 (paperback) | ISBN 9781938849695 (e-book)
Subjects: | GSAFD: Mystery fiction. | Suspense fiction.
Classification: LCC PS3569.U896 H43 2016 | DDC 813/.54--dc23
LC record available at https://lccn.loc.gov/2016020626

HEARTATTACK AND VINE, written by Tom Waits
© 1980 JALMA MUSIC (ASCAP) for USA and Fifth Floor Music Inc. (ASCAP) for Canada. Lines from song used by permission. All rights reserved.

Cover design by Howard Grossman
Book layout and design by Amy Inouye
Printed in the United States of America

ALSO BY PHOEF SUTTON

To my daughters, Skylar and Celia,
the brightest stars in my sky

"Don't you know there ain't no devil,
there's just God when he's drunk"

—"Heartattack and Vine," Tom Waits

BROADWAY

CHAPTER ONE

April, Three Years Ago

I hate LA," Rachel said as she traced a thin black line with her paintbrush onto the white tile that lined the face of the Feingold's Deli stall in bustling Grand Central Market. "What I love is Los Angeles."

She pronounced it with a hard "g," the way people did in the 1930s. "Los Ang-a-lees." With her short-cropped hair, bleached a platinum blond, and her white blouse, Rachel looked like she could have been an extra in an old gangster movie herself. Only the Bluetooth headset clipped to her ear and the snake tattoo on her arm spoiled the illusion.

"I hate the new Hollywood Boulevard. And I hate what they're doing to Los Feliz and West Hollywood and all the faux-hip shops in Silver Lake," she said as she continued to paint graffiti on the front of Feingold's. "What I love is downtown Los Angeles, in all its messy glory. That's the real City of Angels, Crush."

Crush was the street name of Caleb Rush. Crush was sitting at a table in front of the Sticky Rice stall, munching on a mess of smelly fried smelt with dipping sauce, Bluetooth nestled in his ear, chatting with Rachel over the airwaves, watching her from the corner of his eye so as not to make it too apparent that they were talking to each other. Rachel was paying good coin for Crush to keep an eye on her, and that's what Crush was doing.

"God, I hate hipsters," Rachel said with a sigh. "They're ruining this town." Crush grunted an agreement while he half-watched her trace retro-style sketches of deli sandwiches on Feingold's façade—graffiti made to order.

Rachel Fury was in her early twenties. With her black eyeliner and blue nail polish, she looked like a poster child for the hipster generation. *No one hates hipsters more than hipsters*, Crush thought. Rachel was a part-time artist, part-time actress, and full-time grifter.

"We're the last of a dying breed, Crush," she said, using his nickname. Crush was ambivalent about the name, but he still answered to it.

"What breed is that?" he asked.

"Hired guns."

"I don't use a gun."

"Neither do I," Rachel said. "I meant it metaphorically. My guns are my brushes. My guns are my way with words. Oh, and my dark, mysterious eyes. Those are my guns, too."

"Okay," Crush said, just to pass the time. "What are my guns?"

"Your guns are you, Crush. You're your own guns."

Crush dipped some more fish in the spicy sauce and took in his surroundings. Grand Central Market was the innards of Los Angeles. The stomach and lower intestines of the town. A city block, sandwiched between the faded glory of the Million Dollar Theatre and Mexican shops that sold votive candles and statues of saints. Recently renovated, the market housed under one roof dozens of stalls featuring everything anyone would want to eat, drink, or ingest. There were delis frequented by thirty-year-old Jews and taco stands where Mexican immigrants actually ate. There were stalls that sold traditional Chinese medicine, kept in dusty vials that looked like they had been there since the turn of the last century. There were trendy hot spots for trendy hipsters, like kombucha bars and artisanal-chocolate shops.

On one side was Broadway, but not the bustling Broadway of New York—the run-down, seedy Broadway of LA. On the other side, the market opened onto the hillside that was once Bunker Hill but was now just the funicular railway called Angel's Flight, whose slanted cars took the trip up the steep route to California Plaza and the swooping walls of Disney Hall—that is, when they weren't closed for safety reasons, which they usually were.

"Mark my words, Crush," Rachel said. "In two years all the old, dirty, sleazy storefronts in this place are going to be closed, and there'll be nothing but latte shops, organic cheeses, and pressed-juice stands. It's the way of the world."

Someone walking through the crowded aisles between the market stands caught Crush's eye and made the hair on his arms stand up. It wasn't that the man was particularly threatening. He was tall and slender, with neatly groomed hair, a gray sportcoat, and an attaché case, like a time traveler from the sixties. The way he looked around with hooded eyes, as if he were a predator seeking prey, sent a warning signal to Crush.

"Principal is approaching," Crush said into his headset with practiced calmness.

Rachel got excited. "Groovy," she said, putting her brush in a jar of water on the counter and waiting for the man to come up to her. "Meet you back at my apartment." She pulled the Bluetooth headset from her ear.

Crush reached in the pocket of his black hoodie and checked the envelope Rachel had given him. He didn't know what was in it. He wasn't being paid to know. He was just being paid to make the transfer. Getting up and throwing the leavings of the fried fish away, he walked over to the deli stand and made as if he were looking at the little blackboard with the daily specials, pointedly ignoring Rachel, who stood next to him, washing out her brushes and singing "California Dreaming" softly to herself.

Sportcoat sidled up to Rachel and backed her into the counter in a way that was both casual and threatening. "Hello, Bridget."

So Rachel was "Bridget" to Sportcoat. Interesting. She'd been Rachel Fury to Crush for as long as he could remember, but at the Nocturne, the nightclub where Crush was a bouncer on the weekends, she was "Layla Lowenstein." A girl like Rachel made up a new identity to fit every occasion.

"Do you have it?" Sportcoat said, letting his briefcase thud like a pendulum against the deli counter.

Crush came up to Sportcoat and tapped him on the shoulder. Not in a particularly aggressive way. Caleb Rush was six-foot-five, two hundred and fifty pounds of muscle, in a tight black T-shirt and hoodie. His clean-shaven head had a nasty scar running from above his left eye across his skull. He didn't have to act aggressively. His physical presence was threat enough.

"You're not dealing with her," Crush said. "You're dealing with me. I have what you want."

Sportcoat looked at Crush and tried very hard not to

look intimidated. "That wasn't part of the deal," he said, reaching into the pocket of his jacket and putting his hand on an object that Crush thought might be a gun.

"It's part of the deal now," Crush said, in an even tone. "Come on." If Sportcoat had a gun, that meant he was expecting trouble, but he'd have been expecting trouble from Rachel, not from a mean piece of a work like Crush.

As he often did, Crush wondered what the hell he had gotten himself into. He was a part-timer himself, and one of his trades was doing odd jobs for friends and family. Rachel was one of those. She'd asked him to handle the transfer of an unnamed object to an unnamed buyer. Rachel was infamous for her transactions, usually of stolen or illegally obtained merchandise. Crush had no moral objections to Rachel's deals, legitimate or otherwise. She was family, sort of, and her money was good. End of story.

But the first thing he had to do was get Sportcoat away from Rachel and out of this crowd of people. If Sportcoat was going to use his gun, Crush wanted him alone, with no bystanders, innocent or otherwise. Crush turned and walked through the crowd, not looking back to see if Sportcoat was following. Crush was willing him away.

Walking to a side exit tucked away between a cheese store and a coffee shop, Crush pushed through a door and into a small hallway lit by flickering fluorescent light. The hallway felt small and dingy after the roomy cacophony of the market. He heard footsteps clicking behind him. A man's step. Crossing to another door, Crush swung it open and entered a dark corridor. Its walls were covered with red floral wallpaper, faded and peeling, a relic of a gaudier, flashier past. They had entered the neighboring building, the illustrious Million Dollar Theatre.

Built in 1918 by Sid Grauman and designed by Albert Martin, it was LA's first grand movie palace. A mad mix of Spanish Colonial and Churrigueresque fantasy, it had stood for nearly a hundred years, doing service as a movie theater, a jazz club, a Mexican vaudeville house, and a Spanish-language church. Now it stood empty, waiting for a savior or a wrecking ball.

Walking through the dark wings of the theater, Crush headed onto the stage in front of the tattered movie screen. His way was lit by a ghost light—a single bulb in a small wire cage set on a pole in the middle of the stage. The ghost light was a theatrical tradition, an offering to the twin show business deities of superstition and safety.

The theater was inky dark and silent, a cathedral to the business of motion picture exhibition. The vast expanse of seats lay before Crush like an unexplored cavern, and the proscenium rose high above him. Longhorn skulls and Aztec gods stared down from the ornate arch. Crush walked several steps past the ghost light and turned around.

Sportcoat was standing about ten feet behind him. The ghost light stood between them like a referee at a prizefight. "Are we there yet?" Sportcoat asked.

"Yes," Crush said. "Do you have the money?"

"Not so fast. Let's get acquainted first. What do they call you?"

"Busy," Crush said. "Let's get this done."

"Okay, Busy," Sportcoat said. "Mr. Emmerich just calls me 'Bub.' "

Mr. Emmerich? He said the name as if Crush should be familiar with it. He didn't know Crush was just a hired intermediary, and Crush wasn't about to clue him in.

"All right, Bub." Unzipping his hoodie, Crush pulled the package out. It was a plain manila envelope, flat and unimpressive. "Do you have the money or not?"

"I have it." Bub set the briefcase down on the wooden stage. "Shall we count three and push?"

"Do we really have to?"

"Mr. Emmerich is fond of ceremony."

"All right," Crush said, crouching down and placing the envelope on the stage. "One, two, three."

Crush slid the envelope across to Bub, and Bub slid the briefcase to Crush. Grabbing the briefcase, Crush opened it and saw that it was filled with bundles of twenty-dollar bills. A lot of bundles. There must have been a hundred thousand dollars in there. Rachel was only paying Crush five hundred to make this exchange. His roommate was right—he really had to start being a better businessman.

He looked up to see Bub examining the contents of the envelope Crush had given him. "Doesn't seem worth it," he said. "But like Grandma used to say, it takes all kinds of crazy people to make a crazy world."

"Your grandma was a smart woman," Crush said.

"You wouldn't say that if you met my grandpa."

Crush shut the briefcase and stood up. The transaction was complete. No gunplay had been necessary. He considered that a success.

"Now," Crush said, "I leave first. You follow."

"Whatever you say."

It didn't really make any difference who led and who followed, but Crush knew that it did matter that he stayed in charge. He walked, covering the distance between them in firm, steady strides. A thought occurred to him when he was opposite the ghost light. He stopped, set the briefcase down on the stage, and opened it.

The bundles of cash looked impressive. He picked one up and flipped through it, like a magician rifling through a deck of cards. The top two bills were real American money. The rest of the bundle was made of cut-up newspaper.

He glanced up at Bub. And at the gun in his hand.

"You had to look, didn't you?" Bub asked.

"I really did. Was this your idea or Mr. Emmerich's?" Crush gestured to the newspaper money.

"Mr. Emmerich thought it would be funny. I'm going to walk away now," Bub said. "You're not going to follow me. Is that understood?"

"Of course. There's no need anyway."

Bub turned to walk off. Then he turned back. "What do you mean?"

"You know Bridget," Crush said. "If Mr. Emmerich cheated her, don't you think she planned on cheating him?"

Bub eyed Crush. "Go on."

"Do you really think that's the genuine article you have in your hand?" Crush had no idea what the genuine article was, of course, but he was pretty sure that whatever Rachel was selling was fake. It was just her way.

Bub maneuvered the manila envelope open again and looked at the contents. Crush could see that they looked like old government documents, marked with a rubber stamp in red ink. Bub licked his thumb and rubbed the red marking. His thumb left a bloody red smear.

"It's a fake!" he said, affronted.

"That's fake. These are fake," Crush said, pointing to the bundles in the attaché case. "We're even."

"I don't think Mr. Emmerich will see it that way," Bub said. "You picked the wrong man to fuck with."

"I didn't pick anybody. I'm just a delivery man."

"We both know better than that." Bub walked closer and kicked the attaché case closed. "Pick it up for me."

"There's a couple of hundred real dollars in there," Crush said. "Don't I get to keep that?"

"Shut up," he said, gesturing with the gun. "You're lucky I don't shoot you right now."

Crush latched the attaché case and handed it to Bub, who leaned forward to take it. When he bent down, Crush grabbed the ghost light and smashed it down on Bub's head. The light bulb burst and the theater went black, but Crush didn't need to see. He grasped Bub where he knew his wrist was and twisted it back. Bub hissed in pain and slammed the back of his head hard into Crush's face.

Crush took the force of the blow, stumbled back, and then gripped Bub's wrist more tightly and twisted it. He heard a satisfying crunch as the joint snapped. Bub groaned, and his gun discharged in a loud explosion off into the wings. Crush spun Bub around, stepped back, and delivered a kick to his chest.

By now, Crush's eyes had adjusted to the dark, so he could make out shapes and shadows. He could just see Bub flying back and falling off the stage into the greater blackness below. Pulling his cell phone from the back pocket of his jeans, he used the flashlight app and located the attaché case where it lay on the stage. Next to it was the envelope Rachel had given him. He picked them both up and walked to the edge of the stage.

Bub was crumpled on the floor, clutching his arm and moaning. The gun was next to him, but he didn't seem to be aware of it. He opened his eyes and looked up at Crush. "What the hell is your problem?"

"I was hired to make an exchange," Crush said, tossing the envelope down at him. "Now I've made it. Take care of yourself." He exited, stage right.

◎

Crush walked around the side of the theater on Third Street, let himself into the little lobby, and stepped onto the elevator. It was a small one, having been installed in the seventies when the building was remodeled. In the 1910s it had been the home of the Department of Water & Power. Back then LA was just another city in California.

He rode up to the fourteenth floor, walked to an apartment and pressed the little black buzzer. Rachel opened the door.

"Well?" she said. "Did you get the cash?" Since he'd seen her, she had dyed her hair a bright red and was drying it with a towel.

"Yes and no," Crush said, walking in. The apartment was small but elaborately furnished. The walls were inlaid with wooden cabinets, and the light fixtures were made of intricate stained glass. "Nice place you have," he said.

"It used to be William Mulholland's office, back in the day."

"What day was that?" Crush said, sitting on a horsehair sofa and setting the attaché case on an old coffee table.

"The bad old days," she said. "Mulholland is the guy who stole water so Los Angeles could grow. In 1918. It's a city founded by pirates, Crush." She tossed her towel on a love seat. "You want a beer? Or a hard cider? Everybody's drinking hard cider now."

"What did they drink in the bad old days?"

"Scotch, I guess."

"Nothing for me," Crush said as he opened the case. The bundles of cash looked glorious.

"Hot damn," Rachel said.

"Don't get too excited," he said, tossing a bundle to her. She flipped through it.

"That bastard," she said when she got to the fake money.

"*You* were cheating *him*," Crush said.

"Yes, but I'm the underdog. They always root for the underdog."

"Who does?"

"The audience."

Crush rubbed his big bald head with his big hand. "Rachel, there's no audience. This isn't a movie."

Rachel shrugged. "It's all a movie, Crush. And I'm the lead. The Manic Pixie Dream Girl, who muddles through life by her wits and her charm, conning rich bad guys out of their ill-gotten gains and winning the heart of the Hunky Good-hearted Bodyguard Action Hero."

"Who's going to play you?"

Rachel looked offended. "Me, of course. They're holding out for Zooey Deschanel, but I think she's too old. The Rock will play you, of course."

"I'd prefer Channing Tatum. Who am I again?"

"You're the bodyguard, stupid."

"I don't recall you winning my heart. That would be kind of creepy, wouldn't it? Given our relationship?"

"We'll change the backstory. We have to work a

romance into it. Give the audience what it wants."

"What if you're not the heroine? What if you're the villain?"

"An anti-heroine?" She shook her head. "Sounds like a seventies movie. Directed by Sidney Lumet or somebody like that. Not very current."

"What were you supposed to be selling him?"

She smiled a bright, charming smile. "Letters of Transit."

"I need more."

"Movie memorabilia is a big collectible item these days. You know, the ruby slippers from *The Wizard of Oz*. The black bird from *The Maltese Falcon*. Rosebud from *Citizen Kane*. Have you seen any of these movies, Crush?"

"I drop by the Cinematheque occasionally."

"Have you seen *Casablanca*?"

" 'We'll always have Paris.' "

"That's the one. Do you remember the Letters of Transit? The secret documents that Peter Lorre gave Humphrey Bogart? The ones Bogart gave Ingrid Bergman at the end so she could leave Casablanca?"

"You forgot to say 'spoiler alert.' "

"After seventy years you get a pass," she said. "Anyway, I'm selling that prop." She opened a drawer in her coffee table, took out ten envelopes, and laid them on the table. "The original Letters of Transit." She took out a Marlboro Light and lit it with a match that she scraped against the tile fireplace.

"Those things will kill you," Crush said.

"A lot of things will kill me. Anyway, I sold them to three collectors yesterday. I've got six more on the hook."

Crush looked at the envelopes. "Are any of them real?"

Rachel looked at Crush as if he'd just said he believed

in Santa Claus. "There *are* no real Letters of Transit. It was just a plot device the screenwriters made up. It's all pretend."

"But are any of them the original prop from the movie?"

She considered for a moment, then opened another drawer. "These two. One was for long shots. The other one is the gold mine. What they call the 'hero' prop. The one for close-ups." She took a long, thin envelope, weathered and stained and marked CONFIDENTIAL SECRET. Undoing the flap on top, she slid out two pieces of paper covered in typewritten French and marked with various official-looking stamps. "It's glorious. A real piece of the dream. Worth maybe a hundred thousand."

"Where did you get it?"

"I borrowed it."

"You stole it."

"Stealing involves keeping. I borrowed it from a collector."

"Did this borrowing involve breaking and entering?"

"I just needed it to make these copies." She opened one of the other envelopes and pulled out a nearly identical copy. "Pretty good, huh? I arranged to sell it nine times over."

"You should have used higher-quality ink. It smeared."

Rachel started. "Shit. Does he know?"

"Bub? Yes. I imagine Mr. Emmerich knows by now."

"Well, shoot," she said. She got up and started collecting her things. "I wanted to sell those other six before anybody found out."

"So now what are you going to do?"

"Disappear. Move to another city. Change my name."

"You think that will be enough? Mr. Emmerich sounds like a dangerous man."

"He's rich and he's mean and his name's not Emmerich."

"What is his name?"

She looked at Crush like she was thinking something over. Then she picked up the real Letters of Transit and handed them to him. "Take these."

"I thought you were going to return them."

"Change of plan," she said. "Just keep them safe. You'll hear from me in two years."

"Why two years?"

"Because that's what it always says: 'Two years later.' Right after the dissolve. That's when you find out what happens to the heroine."

"The Manic Pixie Dream Girl?"

"That's right. When she goes off to find herself. Without the Letters of Transit or any evidence to tie her down." She pulled her car keys out of her pocket. "Do you want a Mini Cooper?"

"You don't need a car?"

"Not where I'm heading. It makes a better story. 'She arrived in New York with nothing but the clothes on her back and twenty dollars in her purse.'"

"And how much in the lining of her jacket?"

"A couple of hundred thou. But that'll be our little secret." She grabbed her jacket. "Take care of yourself, Crush. When you see me again, I'll be on top of the world."

Rachel kissed him on the head and was gone, leaving the door of the apartment wide open. She didn't care. She wasn't coming back.

◉

Crush thought of her often over the next few years. When he heard of an unidentified body being discovered in the Angeles National Forest, he wondered if it might be her. It wasn't. He told K.C. Zerbe, his roommate and half-brother, to search for her occasionally on the internet. He turned up nothing.

So Crush just kept the Letters of Transit hidden in a safe behind a poster in his loft and three Christmases rolled by. The crowd at the nightclub where Crush worked as a bouncer drank and danced and aged three years under his watchful eye. It was January and the Oscar nominations were the hot topic, everyone calling up the list on their mobile devices and discussing which of the movies they'd seen and which they'd only heard about. Crush, standing against the wall and being invisible like a good bouncer, hadn't seen or heard of any of the films. He didn't keep in touch with pop culture.

One of the nightclubbers shoved an oversized cell phone in front of his nose and asked him what he thought. He was about to shrug and say he didn't think about it much at all when he saw a photo of the Best Supporting Actress nomination for an up-and-coming young star named Rachel Strayhorn. Take away her sandy blond hair and her blue eyes and she was a dead ringer for Rachel Fury.

Once a con artist, always a con artist, thought Crush.

BLUE JAY WAY

CHAPTER TWO

February, Present Day

Three years passed before he saw her again, not two. That was one of the few miscalculations Crush had ever known Rachel to make. It was a Thursday night at the club, but that didn't mean things were quiet. As Gail, the bartender who had recently been promoted to week-night manager, put it: Thursday was the new Friday. The night when you could cut loose at the end of a long week, even if the week wasn't quite over. Friday didn't really count as a workday anymore. It was just a prelude to the weekend.

The nightclub was just off Melrose, in the heart of what used to be the genuine punk-rock scene of LA and was now the touristy-ironic-post-punk-rock scene of LA. The Nocturne had been around for twenty years, which practically qualified it for historic landmark status in Los Angeles County. It had gone through a lot of incarnations in that time. Chaz Pomerantz, the owner, believed that a business had to reinvent itself every three years to survive, so he had run through practically every theme imaginable in the past decades, from Disco Nostalgia to Victorian Opulence to *Mad Men* Chic. This season the décor was Prohibition Era Speakeasy, complete with a hidden entrance in the back of a barbershop storefront.

It was *the* place to be this winter. Chaz was already planning the next makeover. A retro–postapocalyptic–*Mad Max* look. He assured everyone it would be the next big thing.

Crush stood by the player piano running his eye over the porkpie-hat-and-cloche-wearing crowd, looking for trouble or potential trouble. Things had been pretty quiet tonight. Only a couple of drunk USC students and an NBC intern blowing off steam. Not enough to make Crush move from his station and throw the offenders out. It was half past midnight, a half hour from closing time, when his cell phone vibrated. He pulled it from his back pocket and checked the number. It was his roommate and sort-of-brother, K.C. Zerbe.

"You're late," Crush said.

"What do you mean?" Zerbe asked.

"You always call at midnight."

"I don't always call."

"Only every night. For the past three years."

"I'm sure I've missed some nights."

"Maybe a few. What's up? I'm busy."

"Busy doing nothing?"

"That's what they pay me for. To know when to do something."

"That's very deep," said Zerbe. "Help me out. I've finished binge-watching."

"Binge-watching what?"

"Everything. Every fucking thing. Now what do I do?"

"Read a book."

"Very funny."

Zerbe was often bored, being trapped as he was within the four walls of the loft he shared with Caleb Rush. A few years back, Zerbe had been convicted on various

charges including insider trading, corporate malfeas-
ance, and violating the Computer and Abuse Act. To hear
Zerbe tell it, he had been set up as the scapegoat by the
higher-ups who got off scot-free and went laughing all
way to the Cayman Islands. And Zerbe? He served three
years in prison before being paroled on account of his
good behavior and on account of California's prisons being filled to the gills. The terms of his parole were simple:
an electronic tether would keep him within the walls he
shared with Crush for the next three years. That room,
overlooking MacArthur Park, was his new prison. It was
better than San Quentin, no question. But it still wasn't
freedom. And it was damn tedious. Two years were left
on his sentence, assuming he didn't fuck it up. Zerbe had
a history of fucking up.

"I don't know what to tell you. Just live your life,"
Crush said.

"That's even funnier."

Crush was distracted by the sound of commotion
from the outside. Ivan, the Russian émigré who manned
the front door, came barging in. "There is problem," Ivan
said in his thick Ukrainian accent. "In parking lot."

"What problem?"

Ivan shrugged. "My English is not so good. A disturbance? A scuffle? A melee?"

"Your English sounds fine to me," Crush said. "Can't
you handle it?"

"I'm paid to man the door," Ivan said. "You're paid to
handle trouble."

Crush clicked off his call and walked quickly out
through the "secret door" and the fake barbershop, on to
the street. The night air was bracing after the close con-
fines of the nightclub and Crush took a deep breath. He

turned toward the parking lot where a mob of people was gathered around a new-model Porsche that had stopped, slant-wise, across three parking places. The crowd was pushing and shoving and yelling.

"Are you sure that's her?" one girl asked.

"That's not her," another answered.

"That *is* her," another argued back. "I'm telling you!"

It didn't look quite like a melee, but then Crush wasn't sure what a melee was. Still, it needed to be taken care of. He pushed onlookers aside until he got to the core of the trouble. Six guys were using their cell phones to take pictures of the driver's seat of the Porsche, elbowing each other out of the way, taking swings at each other with their fists, trying to get the best view of the inside of the sports car.

Crush grabbed the first lookie-loo he came across and shoved him up against the silver roof of the Porsche, so he could get a good look at the source of all this madness. The driver's door was open and a young woman was sprawled in the seat, unconscious with her mouth open, with a glistening line of drool running down her chin.

In any other pose this would have been a remarkably attractive woman and even in this condition she looked damned good. A lovely young thing done up to look cheap and tawdry, in the style of media stars of the day. Heavy eye makeup, obviously dyed blond hair, a nose stud, and ruby red lips. She wore a very short, very expensive dress that was hiked up around her hips.

But it wasn't what she was wearing that was garnering all the attention. It was what she wasn't wearing. Panties. That explained the many pictures that were being taken. Oscar-nominated Rachel Strayhorn was a movie star and it wasn't often you saw a movie star's snatch in person, let alone got to take a picture of it.

Crush grabbed the cell phone from the young guy he held against the Porsche and threw it to the ground. "Didn't your mother teach you that private parts are private?" he barked.

Another creep took another picture. Crush grabbed his cell phone and threw it over his shoulder onto the pavement.

"Hey, that phone cost me a hundred dollars," the creep objected.

"Then you shouldn't have taken those pictures," Crush said.

"I still have the pictures, dude," the creep laughed. "They got sent to my Cloud."

Crush thought about punching him out but decided that it wouldn't accomplish anything. The photos had drifted off to everybody's iClouds and Dropboxes, had been sent off to relatives and friends, to TMZ and Perez Hilton. The genie was out of the bottle.

He bent down to examine the girl in the Porsche. Lifting her eyelid with his thumb, he watched her eye roll in its socket as if she was riding high on some kind of designer drug. He cursed under his breath and picked her up. Pulling her out of the car, he slung her over his shoulder, remembering to tug her short skirt down to cover her ass. He carried her through the crowd, back around the building, to the employees' entrance.

The back room of the club was dingy and musty and hadn't been remodeled since the nineties. He dumped her on the ratty sofa and a cloud of dust flew up. He shut the door and, averting his eyes, he pulled her skirt down once again. Crush leaned against the wall and sighed. "What the hell are you trying to pull, Rachel?"

Her eyes opened. They looked alert, clear, and not the least bit high. She smiled at Crush. "It's a long con, Crush. A very long con."

Crush sighed again. There were two stories behind this girl and Crush knew both of them.

One was the story of Rachel Strayhorn. The young movie star of the moment. The story everyone knew. Rachel had burst upon the scene only a year ago, in a supporting role in Adam Udell's *Winter of Our Discontent*. Her performance as a drugged-out hooker stole the picture from George Clooney and Gwyneth Paltrow. And just three weeks ago, *The Rage Machine*, also directed by Adam Udell, had opened, breaking box office records and proving with her starring performance that Rachel could "open a picture," in the language of the movie business. To cap it off, a couple of weeks ago she was nominated for an Oscar for Best Supporting Actress for *Discontent*. Her rise had been meteoric.

Meteoric too had been her journey through the media firestorm. First off, everybody loved her. After all, she came out of nowhere. Folks saw her as the underdog who upstaged Gwyneth Paltrow. Who couldn't like her for that?

The backlash started a mere two weeks later. She was just a flash in the pan, the haters said. The flavor of the week. When it came out that she was sleeping with the director of her two films, wunderkind hipster Adam Udell, she was roundly condemned. Adam had a longtime girlfriend named Polly Coburn, and Rachel was seen as a home-wrecker who used her feminine wiles to land good parts in Adam's movies. And couldn't anybody have done well with those plum roles?

Then the inevitable sex tape went viral. Rachel paired

with an unknown stud, leaving only a little to the imagination. People called her a slut and a gold digger. People actually started to feel sorry for that asshole Adam Udell, which was an amazing feat in itself.

By now the backlash to the backlash was starting, and people were feeling sorry for her. Rachel was yet another victim of the pressures of fame. These pictures in the parking lot would be just fuel for the fire.

Crush opened the fridge. "You still like Dr Pepper?" he asked her.

"Once a Pepper always a Pepper," she said. She sounded sharp and sober. Whatever drug had made her pass out behind the wheel was not in evidence now.

He popped open a can and handed it to her. She drank deep. "You always did know how to make an entrance," he said.

"Do you think?" she said. "I was worried maybe the drooling was a little much."

"You worried about the drooling but you didn't worry about being bare-assed for all the world to see?"

"Being bare-assed is a part of the con. Although I admit, I was a little embarrassed about you seeing my coochie, Big Brother."

"Don't call me that."

"Aren't you my big brother? Didn't your mother marry my dad?"

"We've never been sure about that."

"Well, you were my big brother in spirit, Crush."

"I guess I was. Maybe that's why I feel the urge to ground you."

She laughed. It was a musical laugh. A charming laugh. Not like the bray she had when she was a kid. It must have taken her months to perfect that laugh. Her voice was different, too. Lower pitched and throatier. Like Angelina Jolie or Lauren Bacall. She had to have worked on that also. "Do you want to know what all this is about?" she asked him.

Crush shook his head. "I really don't."

"You're not curious?"

"I got over being curious a long time ago. Makes life simpler."

"I need you to take me somewhere."

"You have a car. You can go anywhere you want."

"That's true. But there are complications."

"And you haven't seen them coming?"

She seemed to take that as a compliment. "It's true, I see all the complications inherent in a con, but this isn't a part of the con. An unforeseen element has forced its way in."

"An unforeseen element?"

"I have my very own stalker," she said with a smile.

"Congratulations, I guess you *are* a star."

"I know, cool, huh?" She sat up on the sofa, excited. "He sends me letters. Says we're married. Says he's going to kill me so no one else can have me. Takes photos of me, does nasty stuff to them, then mails them to me."

"And you think he's serious?"

"I get that feeling."

"And yet you still lay out there in that Porsche, half naked, where anybody can grab you?"

"That's a part of the con. I can't deviate from the con."

He could see her point. He almost asked what the con was, but then he realized he was playing right into her hands. Clever girl, Rachel. "What do you want me to do about it?"

"Aren't you a security guard?"

He shook his head. "Not anymore. I'm just a bouncer."

"Won't you guard your little sister?" Rachel said with a little girl's pout. Really, she was laying it on pretty thick.

Just then Gail walked in. "What's holding you up, Crush? It's last call." A bouncer was most necessary at last call, rounding up the malingerers and letting them know that they didn't have to go home, but they had to go somewhere else.

Catherine Gail, with her long, unruly mane of black hair and dark, piercing eyes, looked like the negative image of Rachel, Crush thought. She was the opposite of Rachel in many other ways, too. If Rachel was Crush's baby sister, Gail was his older sister. More than his boss, she was his mentor. His sensei. She was the one who'd set him on the straight and narrow, after he'd hit rock bottom. She'd led him to AA. She was his tae kwon do master and his best friend. Nearly everyone who knew them thought they were lovers, but their relationship was far too complex to allow for that.

Gail did a double take when she saw Rachel Strayhorn in the flesh, sitting in the back room. Crush had never seen her so impressed. "Well, hello!" she said. "Are you who I think you are?"

"I think I am," Rachel said with a charming smile she must have spent hours in the mirror perfecting.

"I loved you in that movie," Gail said.

"Thank you."

"And you were great in that other one, too." Crush had never seen Gail starstruck before. He didn't think it suited her.

"I'm just here catching up with an old friend," Rachel said, gesturing toward Crush.

"You never told me you knew Rachel Strayhorn," Gail said to Crush.

"I knew her before she was Rachel Strayhorn. When she was just Rachel Fury."

"That's the nice thing about being an actress," Rachel said. "You can change your name and nobody thinks twice."

"I think Rachel Fury is a nice name," Gail said.

Rachel grimaced. "It sounds too made-up. Besides, I've left that life behind. You know what they say, it's never too late to have a happy childhood."

"And you're having one now?" Gail asked.

"Oh, I'm having a blast," Rachel replied. "You should try being famous sometime. You get everything for free and people let you get away with murder."

"Sounds like it would be pretty great," Gail said. "For a while. But I like being anonymous."

"Yeah, you have to give that up," Rachel admitted. "And sometimes nuts try to kill you for no reason. But other than that it's dope."

Gail cast an inquisitive look toward Crush. "She has a stalker," he explained.

"Seriously?"

"An occupational hazard," Rachel explained. "I asked Crush to protect me, but he says he doesn't do that kind of work anymore."

"Did you say that?" Gail asked Crush.

"I said that," he said. "I have a job, remember? I work for you."

"It's closing time, Caleb," Gail said. "You're off the clock. Why don't you help her out?"

"See, you have to listen to your public," Rachel said to him. "And I only need protection for tonight. After that

I'm off to New Orleans to start shooting the *Rage* sequel."

"Really?" Gail asked, impressed. "No spoiler alerts, but do you survive?"

"I haven't read the script yet."

"She's joking, right?" Gail asked Crush.

"I have no idea. Are you joking, Rachel?"

"Could be."

"If she only needs you for tonight, Caleb, why can't you do it?" Gail asked. "I mean, if she's an old friend."

"Yeah, why can't you, Crush?" Rachel said, all wide-eyed and innocent.

"I wouldn't call us old friends," Crush said. "We were more like..."

"Accomplices?" Rachel said.

"I was going to say partners, but you get the idea," Crush said. He knew when he was beat. He also had to admit he was curious to find out what Rachel's con was. "Okay, we'll take your car," Crush said.

"You mean you'll be my guardian angel?" Rachel was smiling that smile again.

"I'll be your security. Where are we going anyway?"

"To my director Adam Udell's place," she said. "His girlfriend is throwing him a birthday party."

"Won't that be awkward?" Gail asked.

"This is Hollywood, honey," Rachel said, as if that explained everything. "Awkward is *so* twentieth century."

CHAPTER THREE

Just getting out to her car was an adventure. The crowd in the parking lot had grown larger in the twenty minutes they were inside and it reacted like a living organism when Crush and Rachel walked out. Reaching out at them like an octopus, crying out like a flock of crows, cell phones clicking at them like snapping turtles. It was as if they were being attacked by a whole goddamned zoo, Crush thought.

He held her close and had her crouch down as they walked, using his big body as a shield. It was an old bodyguard trick, but it only protected her from the amateur paparazzi. If someone out there really wanted to hurt her then Crush would have to get serious.

Opening the car door, he bent her over and shoved her in, shutting the door and spinning around to glare at the mob that was closing in around him. One glare from Crush and the mob started to disperse. He had a way of clearing a path in front of him with just a cold stare. These were the times he was worthy of his nickname.

He made his way around to the driver's door and got in. "How do they all know you're here anyway?" he asked Rachel, not expecting an answer.

"They follow me on wherearethey.com."

"What's that?" he asked, pressing the ignition button to start the car. He didn't have to borrow the keys from

Rachel. With the wisdom of the twenty-first century, the car knew she was inside.

"It's an app where you can track stars. Follow them. Find out where they are."

"That's scary," he said, pulling out onto Melrose.

"Goes with the territory."

"How does it know where you are?"

"People tell it."

"What kind of people?"

She shrugged. "Fans. Or groupies. Or, in this case, me."

Crush couldn't believe what he was hearing. "You told those nuts where you'd be?"

"They're not nuts. They're my fans. If it weren't for them, I'd be nobody."

"Why would you do that? And then why would you pretend to be drunk and flash them your..."

"It's called a pussy, Crush."

"Why would you do that?"

"Didn't you ever hear there's no such thing as bad publicity? I've set it to post where I am, automatically, every two hours. That way I don't have to remember." She checked her iPhone. "Look, I'm already trending on Twitter."

"You mean, your pussy is trending."

"It's all part of the package."

Crush shook his head. "You were never a slut when I knew you."

"When you knew me I was ten. And what makes you think I'm a slut now?"

"Let me think."

"For your information, I happen to be a virgin."

"Really."

"Yes, I'm saving myself for marriage."

Crush glanced her way. "Would you think I was crazy if I said I half-way believe you?"

"You'd be half-way right, big brother."

◎

The other story behind this girl was the story of Rachel Fury. Crush knew that one, too. Firsthand.

Crush was about to turn twenty when he first met Rachel. He wasn't called Crush yet, but he'd done a lot of living in his nineteen years. He had been a soldier for the Russian mob, he had run numbers, been an enforcer, and even smuggled heroin. But he'd never seen eyes as calculating and shrewd and downright scary as the ones that met his in the rearview mirror from the back seat of the beat-up old Chrysler he was driving down Highway 58 outside Bakersfield. Rachel Fury was the hardest, most stone-cold motherfucker he had ever been paired with. And she was only ten years old.

They were getting ready to play the swoop and squat. Caleb was scanning the traffic to spot a potential mark. Someone driving responsibly, obeying all the traffic laws. Someone with an expensive car, preferably an SUV. Something bigger and more powerful than the dinky Chrysler that Caleb was piloting along the highway.

"Where's your mom?" Rachel asked him.

He checked the side mirror. "She's back there."

"I hope she knows what she's doing," Rachel said. "Poppa's last girlfriend, Brenda, she was a master at the swoop. She'd cut in and cut out like she was never there."

"And where's she now?" Caleb asked.

"Doing five years in Chowchilla," Rachel said. "She sends me cards sometimes."

"That's nice."

"I like you," Rachel said. "But I don't like your name. What kind of mother gives somebody a name like Caleb?"

"She was going through a biblical phase."

Caleb switched lanes so that he was in front of a minivan being driven by a meek-looking soccer mom. Very different, Caleb thought, from his own mother, who never drove a carpool in her life. There were no kids in the minivan though. Caleb made sure of that. Kids in the mark's car only complicated matters.

"What you need is a street name," Rachel said. "Did you ever have a street name, Caleb?"

"My father called me Vikenty."

"What's that mean?"

"It's Russian for 'conqueror.'"

"Why did he call you that?"

"I was big for my age. I used to win fights."

"Who'd you fight with?"

"My older brothers. He thought it was funny to sic them on me and see how I'd do."

"Your father sounds like a sweet guy."

"I didn't mind. It kept me on my toes."

"Why'd they split up? Your mom and him?"

"He beat her. I tried to persuade him not to do that. With a baseball bat."

"I'd like to have seen that."

"I didn't hurt him bad, I just made my point. But after that, we had to run. Russian mob leaders don't take kindly to being beaten up by fifteen-year-old boys."

A Mustang was coming from behind on his left. That was his mother, Toni, driving the swoop car. She'd never worked this con before, but Caleb knew she'd do her part well. His mom was the definition of a quick study.

◉

Toni Rush was born Francine Russo across the country in Brighton Beach, New York, an area better known as Little Odessa. She was an independent kid with inattentive parents, so from the age of fourteen on she was living pretty much on her own. She wasn't Russian but she started running with the Russian kids as soon as she could run.

At fifteen, she had changed her name to Toni Rush and was the steady girlfriend of a Ukrainian pimp named Dimitri. Dimi tried to get her to "go on the life," but she told him to fuck off, so he beat her up pretty badly.

His boss, Blaz Kusinko, the kingpin of the Russian mob from Ocean Parkway to Sheepshead Bay, saw this and felt sorry for her. He took her in and started looking after her, and when Dimitri objected, Blaz had him taken away and Toni never saw him again. After that, Toni became one of Blaz's "exclusives," and everybody knew to keep their hands off her. He treated her well at first, and if he had other girlfriends, well, Toni knew that went with the territory. She liked being royalty, liked the sense that everyone was a little afraid of her because she was Blaz's property.

All of that changed when she had Caleb. She was sixteen by then, older and wiser. Somehow when she held him in her arms the first time, she realized she mattered. This squirming, crying thing was depending on her to keep it alive. That was serious shit. From that moment on, it was Toni and Caleb against the world.

Blaz had other sons, of course, from other women. They ran in a pack around him, and he delighted in the

mayhem they caused, but he didn't pay particular attention to any of them—he just loved to watch them tussle.
After a few years, he noticed that one boy was bigger and
tougher than the rest. That one could beat even the older
boys in the ring.

By the time Caleb was fifteen, he was one of Blaz's
favored sons. Blaz already had him out doing odd jobs,
running numbers, making drops, even going along on the
occasional enforcement job. Toni watched this with wary
approval, glad that Caleb had become a favorite, but worried where that might lead. So when she heard Blaz ask
Caleb if he thought he was "capable," she knew she had
to do something.

"Capable" was Mob-speak for someone willing and
able to kill.

So she waited until she could speak to Blaz privately
and then she told him all the reasons that she didn't
want Caleb to be a killer. He listened patiently, nodded
gravely, and proceeded to beat the living shit out of her.
He told her quietly and calmly while he was slugging her
that she should stay out of his business and that he'd do
whatever he wanted with that boy. Blaz had made him;
Blaz could destroy him. "It's nature's law," he said. Then
he threw her out in the street.

Caleb found his mother huddled in the alley behind
Blaz's house. She wasn't in any condition to tell him
what happened, but she didn't have to. Caleb grabbed a
baseball bat and went in to talk to his father.

After that they took off and ended up in Southern
California, where Toni got whatever work she could, everything from bagging groceries to exotic dancing. For a
time she was the girlfriend-on-the-side of a big Hollywood
director and even the trophy wife of a wealthy investment

banker in Pasadena. When that marriage went south, she fled to Bakersfield, where she eventually hooked up with Rachel Fury and her dad.

The Furys lived in a trailer park off Wible Road and made a living doing staged car accidents, home repair scams, and bogus fortune-telling. Caleb went along with his mom, though by now their roles were reversed. He was taking care of *her*.

◎

Now Toni was driving a Mustang down Route 58, her blond hair flying in the wind, looking, Caleb thought, like a more mature version of Suzanne Somers from *American Graffiti*. His mother may have gotten older but that hadn't dimmed her charms. Her charms were all she had, and she wasn't about to let them go without a fight.

Toni's Mustang swerved in front of Caleb in the Chrysler. That was his cue. Caleb went into autopilot, hit the brakes, and waited for the satisfying crunch from the impact of the minivan striking them from behind.

The van plowed into them with surprising force. The Chrysler was propelled forward and Caleb spun the wheel so his car went off onto the shoulder. They crashed into the guardrail, and Caleb and Rachel were thrown around in the Chrysler like dice in a cup.

Their car slammed to a stop, and Rachel started crying just like an actual ten-year-old. Caleb opened the car door and fell out onto the street. His shoulder hit the gravel just as the woman from the minivan rushed over.

"My God," she said. "Are you all right?" She had to shout to be heard over Rachel's screaming.

Caleb pushed himself up and looked around. "Rachel?

Where are you?"

"She's in the back seat," the woman said. "She's okay."

"My neck!" Rachel cried. "It hurts!"

The woman helped him up, and Caleb clambered up her arms until he was leaning against her. She looked to be about forty, in mom jeans and a blue cotton sweater. He liked her at once and felt guilty about what they were going to do. But business was business.

"My little sister!" Caleb said. "She's hurt!" He pushed the woman aside and wrenched open the back door. Rachel was writhing in the back seat, clutching her neck and moaning.

"Oh, God," the woman said. "It's all right, honey. Your brother's here."

Caleb climbed in and hugged Rachel, whispering in her ear, "Don't you think you're laying it on a little thick?"

"She's buying it, isn't she?" Rachel whispered back.

"Your sister's okay, right?" The woman's voice was full of concern. Yes, she was buying it.

Caleb came out of the car, his face wracked with worry. "I don't think so."

"She's not really hurt, is she?"

"I have to get her to a hospital."

"Does she need that? It's not that serious, is it?" She poked her head in the back and said to Rachel, "You're not really hurt, are you?"

Rachel moaned. "I can't feel my leg," she said with a sob.

"Oh, my God." The woman turned to Caleb. "I'm so sorry. You just stopped short all of sudden when that car cut you off."

"What car?" Caleb said.

"The car. The Mustang."

"I didn't stop. You rammed into me."

The woman stared at him. "But you stopped short."

"No I didn't." Caleb said it definitively, as if there were no room for argument.

A man wearing a Dodgers cap and a jean jacket rushed up to them and asked, "Is anybody hurt?" He was running from a late-model Ford parked on the shoulder a little ways off.

"My sister needs a doctor," Caleb said urgently.

"I'm not surprised," the man said. "The way she rammed into you."

"She can't feel her leg," the woman said. Rachel moaned louder and Caleb hurried over to her. The woman pulled the guy in the Dodgers cap aside and asked him, "Did you see what happened?"

"I saw the whole thing," the man said. "Were you on your cell phone or something?"

"I wasn't..." The woman was starting to panic. "That car cut him off."

"What car?"

"It wasn't my *fault*."

"You hit him, lady. From behind. I saw the whole thing."

Caleb hurried over to them. He didn't have the scar on his forehead yet and he wasn't bald, but even with a full head of hair and an unmarred face, he cut an intimidating figure. He was a very big boy. "Don't you leave!" he barked at her. "Don't hit and run!"

"What?" the woman was on the defensive. "I'm not running! I'm right here."

"We have to exchange information, right? Insurance? Lawyers?"

"Lawyers?" she asked, her voice trembling.

"Let me get the papers. Then I have to get Rachel to the ER." He hurried off to the Chrysler and started rummaging through the glove compartment.

She turned to the witness. "What does he mean, 'lawyers'?"

The man took off his Dodgers cap and ran his fingers through his gray hair. "He's going to sue you, I guess. Can't say I blame him. If that little girl is really hurt, the medical bills will be through the roof. He's gotta clean you out. He has no other choice."

"But it wasn't my fault."

"It's your word against his," the man said. "And mine, of course."

"And you're sure you didn't see the other car?" She was looking at him with pleading eyes.

"I'm sure." After a pause he added, "Of course, I could be made *less* sure."

"How do you mean?" She looked genuinely confused.

"Look, he's going to ask for hundreds of thousands of dollars. I mean, look at your minivan and look at the junker he's driving. It's going through his head now. You're his meal ticket."

"But it wasn't my fault. You could say that. You could say you saw the other car."

"But I didn't."

"It was there! I could...I could...give you something. Is that what you mean?"

"You want me to lie?"

"You wouldn't be lying. You'd be saying what really happened. Just not what you saw."

He put the Dodgers cap back on and looked at her with a grave expression on his face. "I'm listening," he said. "How much?"

Over at the Chrysler, Caleb was still going through the cluttered glove compartment. After he'd stolen the car, he'd stocked the glove box with a lot of loose paper so he could search through it long enough to let Rachel's father plant the hook.

Caleb checked the side mirror. They were talking intently. "He's got her," he whispered to Rachel.

"Of course he's got her. Dad's the best."

"I feel sorry for her."

"I know what your street name should be, Caleb Rush. I'm gonna call you 'Crush.'"

"I don't think I like that."

"People'll think it's 'cause you're so tough. But you're not. You've got a crush on that soccer mom, don't you? You'll never make it as a grifter, Crush. You're too soft."

"I hope you're right, Rachel."

Later they gathered around in Lloyd Fury's trailer and split up the take over a pitcher of sweet iced tea and a bucket of KFC. Lloyd and Toni were busy planning the rest of their tour around Kern County, and Rachel was saying she was going to use her cut to buy a set of Pokémon cards.

Caleb watched them and reflected that this was one of the few times he had ever shared a real, sit-down family dinner. He would remember it often over the years. How he almost found a home and a family and a little sister.

Almost, but not quite.

◎

Crush glanced over at Rachel Fury, who was now Rachel Strayhorn, as he drove the Porsche down Sunset Boulevard and noticed that she had a new tattoo on the upper part of her left arm. A spider's web. *Very appropriate,* he thought.

"Where are we going?"

She looked up from entering a text into her phone. "His villa in the Hollywood Hills."

"How many villas does he have?"

"Villas or mansions or apartments or cottages or bungalows or pied-à-terres? He's got a lot of them."

"Why?"

She shrugged. "He collects them. He collects a lot of things."

"Must have a lot of time on his hands."

"Yeah. Except when he's directing. And throwing bad movie parties."

"Bad movie parties?"

"Parties where Adam shows any dumbass bad movie he wants and everybody has to say how much they enjoy it. Adam has eclectic taste."

"People like that?"

"As long as the movies he directs make money they like it."

"Is that what this party is?"

"I imagine. His longtime girlfriend is throwing it and she likes to keep him happy. She's sort of the power behind the throne, I guess. They went to film school together. She became his editor and he became...God."

"And she's going to be okay with you showing up?"

"They have an open relationship. But despite what the tabloids say, Adam and I are not lovers. I'm probably the only person, male or female, that Adam Udell hasn't been able to get in the sack. At least since he's become an A-list director."

"So that's your angle?"

She smiled. It was the sly smile Crush knew from the old days. For a second he could almost see the little girl's face superimposed over the woman's. "Adam Udell is like a king in his world. Everything he asks for, he gets. He doesn't even hear the word 'no.' Except from me. That intrigues him."

"What's your end game?"

"I've been waiting for you to ask. I want to marry him."

"That's a pretty tall order."

"Like I said, it's a long con."

"And I suppose you don't want a prenup?"

"Wouldn't be much point in it with a prenup."

"So all this? The movie career, the Oscar nomination, the stalker?"

"Just collateral damage."

"Okay." Crush knew he was hooked. "Tell me the story."

"I met Adam at a nightclub."

"By chance?"

"By chance and a lot of prep work. Caught his eye. Flirted with him. Did a little negging."

Crush nodded. He knew the drill. The seduction trick of giving backhanded compliments, coupling them with insults, and generally undermining the target's confidence. "And that worked?"

"Oh, yeah. People think negging is just effective with women," Rachel went on, "but Adam was so used to yes-men that he ate it up. He asked me to call him. I figured he wanted to get with me, then toss me aside, so I didn't. After a few days, he found my number and *he* called *me*. That was when I knew I had a shot. He said he wanted me for his next movie. I still figured that was a come-on.

Maybe it was, but I got the part.

"And you know what? It turns out being a con artist is a great training ground for an actor. I mean, I'd been in plays and student films before, so I knew my way around a role. But I found I could really get into the character, just like you do when you're playing a mark. Only the mark was the camera. Hell, the mark was the whole world. I convinced them I *was* that person—a drug-addicted prostitute on her way to destruction. It was fun. I liked it. But I never lost sight of my ultimate goal."

"Adam Udell?" he asked as he drove up a long driveway to the sleek midcentury house perched on the hillside.

"That's right."

"But why do you need that? You're a movie star now. Isn't that enough?"

"Crush, if there's one thing I've learned about show business, it's this: no matter how successful you are, never quit your day job."

CHAPTER FOUR

A dam Udell's villa was on Blue Jay Way, one of the exclusive "bird streets" in the Hollywood Hills, home to Leonardo and Keanu and a couple of Jennifers. Blue Jay Way was all the more special since it was immortalized in a rather annoying song by George Harrison.

Crush pulled to the curb a few houses from the villa. Ahead there was a valet parking station and a small crowd of paparazzi, snapping shots of celebrities as they got out of their cars. "They're everywhere," he said.

"They're like the little fish who swim between sharks' teeth and pick off the carrion. It's a very symbiotic relationship."

Crush didn't want to get out of the Porsche and face them right away. "Tell me about your stalker."

"Well, his name is Brandon Renbourn. He's twenty-eight, he's a realtor from Temecula. Oh, here's a picture of himself he sent me." Rachel showed Crush the photo on her iPhone.

"Hmm," he said. "I can't see his face, what with the low angle and his penis blocking it and all."

"Yeah, I sent him a text complaining about that. This was his response." She showed him another picture. This one was of her with her eyes cut out and blood drawn streaming down her face.

"Did you show this to the police?"

"Oh, yes. They put a restraining order on him. So when he kills me, they can slap him on the wrist for breaking it."

"Have you ever seen him in person?"

"Of course. He's at all the clubs, the hotels, the premieres. And I've seen him in court, too. He waved at me and blew me kisses. Here's a better picture of him."

She flipped through to a shot of him on the witness stand, smiling like he knew she was taking a picture of him and wanted to look his best. A big man crammed into a dark suit, with short hair. He reminded Crush a little of Raymond Burr as Perry Mason. He looked harmless enough to be really dangerous.

"Does he know you're coming here tonight?"

"I don't know. But he seems very good at tracking me. Here, he took all these and sent them to me." She showed him a series of photos of herself coming out of restaurants, clubs, even a sauna at a gym. "I'm apparently all he thinks about. I'd be flattered if it wasn't for the psycho-crazy aspect of the thing."

Crush looked toward the paparazzi. "I don't see him. Is that why you want me here?"

"I'm scared, Crush," she said. Crush looked at her, and she looked like she meant it. But, of course, like she had said, she was good at looking like she meant things.

"Stay here," Crush said as he climbed out of the Porsche. No one took pictures of him. He wasn't anybody. He walked up to the house, which was made of white rectangular blocks and looked like Frank Lloyd Wright had designed it on a dare from Richard Neutra. He knocked on the shiny metal door and a window slid open to reveal a large African-American version of Crush. "You have an invitation?" the big man asked in a gravelly voice over the pounding throb of DeadMau5.

"I'm security. For Rachel Strayhorn. Just checking to see if the place is secure."

"Nobody will kill her, if that's what you mean."

"That's what I mean."

Crush went back to the car to find Rachel thumbing her cell phone. "You didn't twit that you were coming here, did you?"

"It's called tweeting," she said. "And, no, I'm just checking my messages."

He plucked the phone from her hands, tossed it into the glove compartment, and drove up to the valet station. He climbed out and walked with Rachel to the front door, keeping an eye out for danger signals and ignoring the flashes and the catcalls from the photographers. "You got an invitation?" he asked her.

"I'm me," she said simply. "That's enough of an invitation."

"Fine. I'll wait out here."

"I'd feel better if you came in with me."

"I'm not your chaperone, Rachel."

"Then what am I paying you for?"

"You're paying me?"

"Sure," she said. "What's your going rate?"

"As much as you can afford," he said, knocking on the door.

The window slid open. "Hey, Lex," she said to the black Crush. "What's tonight's movie?"

"A double feature. *Vanishing Point* and *The Honeymoon Killers.*"

"Groovy," she said.

Opening the door, the big man let her in. Then he locked eyes with Crush. Lex's eyes were at the same level as Crush's, which didn't happen often. Crush looked right back at him. "He's with me," Rachel said.

Lex stepped aside and Crush walked through a small foyer into the wide expanse of the living room. The décor was white walls, white textiles, and blond wood, with a huge spiral staircase that looked like it had been transported from Captain Picard's *Enterprise*. The room looked like it had been assembled two hours earlier by workmen in a "clean room" laboratory of the sort normally reserved for making silicon chips for satellites and rockets. It was filled with beautiful people who appeared to have been built in the same lab.

Rachel led the way through the crowd, which swayed to the beat of the EDM that pounded through the walls like the beating of some huge monster's heart. There were display cases lining the walls, pinpoints of light falling on the contents, as if they were treasures from ancient Egypt.

A pair of tattered boxing gloves. A spaceman's ray gun from the future, circa 1950. A coiled bullwhip, a bit frayed and worn. A bowler hat with a metal rim. The metal skeleton of what looked like a miniature gorilla. A black enameled statue of a bird. A small pistol. A decaying rubber figure that looked like a cross between a human spine and a large caterpillar. The hilt of an electronic sword.

"I know what that is," Crush shouted over the throbbing music. "That's a light saber, right?"

"Luke Skywalker's original. And those are Rocky's boxing gloves. And a ray gun from *Forbidden Planet*. That's Indiana Jones's whip. Odd Job's hat from *Goldfinger*. An original armature from *King Kong*, the 1933 one, of course. That's the Maltese Falcon. James Bond's Walther PPK from *Dr. No.* And a tingler from *The Tingler.*"

Crush recognized most of the movies she'd mentioned. Zerbe was a good influence on his pop culture knowledge. "Impressive," he said.

"It's more than impressive," Rachel said. "Look at this." She led him over to two alcoves set in the wall above the fireplace. In one was a pair of high heels covered with red sequins. In the other was an antique sled.

"Whoa," said Crush.

"That's right. Dorothy's ruby slippers. Rosebud from *Citizen Kane.* He has a lot more in storage."

"But not the Letters of Transit?"

She gave Crush a sideways glance. "No. Not the Letters of Transit." She led him to two ornate double doors set in the far wall and swung them open.

Inside was an elaborate replica of a 1930s movie-theater lobby, complete with costumed ushers and a concession stand stocked with Jujubes, Charleston Chews, and real popcorn bouncing out of a real popcorn machine. As the doors closed, the thumping music from the other room was silenced.

"Very authentic," Crush said.

"It ought to be. He had it moved from an actual theater in El Segundo that was being torn down."

One of the ushers opened the door to the theater itself, and Rachel and Crush walked in. Inside it was dark and a movie was playing. A Dodge Challenger was zooming down a one-lane highway in the desert of the 1970s. Around him, Crush could make out the elaborate décor of a Depression-era version of an Egyptian temple. Over the screen, a sphinx stared down at them with glowing eyes.

Instead of finding a seat, Rachel turned and walked

out. "Barry Newman is racing that Dodge across the desert to California. The cops are after him. And do you know why he's doing it?"

"No. Why?"

"They never say. You didn't need backstory in the seventies."

Rachel opened a sliding glass door that led into the backyard. She walked around the blue-lit infinity pool, which was built to look as if its edge just fell off into the night air. Crush expected it to be full of people, cavorting and splashing, but its waters were calm and empty. There was more fun to be had inside, he decided.

Circling it, Rachel walked over to a man seated at a table overlooking the spectacular view of the city at night. The hill curled around him in a cozy fashion, so it seemed like the nighttime cityscape was just a stage set up for his personal amusement.

Crush recognized the man as film director and professional bad boy Adam Udell. In his mid-thirties, he had fashionably long black hair and a fashionably trimmed beard. He was wearing a black blazer over a black T-shirt on top of black jeans, making him look like a hipster undertaker running a boho funeral parlor, no doubt featuring hand-crafted caskets and artisanal embalming fluid.

Next to him sat a wiry old man who looked to be in his mid-eighties. With the wild shock of white hair falling across his leathery forehead and the Navajo squash-blossom necklace hanging carelessly from his neck, he effortlessly achieved the effect that Adam was striving for. The old guy was cool; Adam Udell was just a wannabe.

The old man crinkled an eye at Rachel as she approached and raised a tumbler of amber liquid in her direction. "Here she comes. Glenda the Good Witch. But where's the bubble you usually ride in on?"

"I left it outside," she said.

The old man opened his mouth in a broad smile and laughed. The laugh didn't make a sound, but a warm and friendly feeling gushed out of him all the same. Crush didn't know who the man was, but he liked him at once. Adam, on the other hand, sniffed ostentatiously and took a sip from a copper mug. Crush felt like slugging him the second he saw him.

"You're taking time out from your busy schedule to put in an appearance at my party? How nice," Adam said.

"I wouldn't miss it for the world," she said. "How come you're out here and not in there?"

Adam shrugged. "It's boring."

The old man let loose another silent laugh. "I told him it would get old. Anything—even your dearest passion—can get tiresome if it's overindulged. Better to take your pleasure in small doses or else you'll find you have nowhere to turn for diversion."

"She doesn't have that problem," Adam said, displaying his iPhone for them. One of the photos of Rachel in the Porsche, legs spread and panties missing, was on display.

"Oh, that," the old man said with a dismissive gesture. "So you can see her muff. Half the world has them, you know. They're no secret."

"But I don't need to see it every time I look at my iPhone," Adam said.

The old man chuckled. "You're just upset because you can look but you can't touch."

"Why don't you go fuck off, Sterling?" Adam said.

"Would that I could," said the old man, whose name was apparently Sterling. "The spirit is willing, but the flesh is limp."

As if to change the subject, Adam looked at Crush with distaste. "I don't remember inviting you, whoever you are."

"He's my bodyguard," Rachel said.

Adam ran his eyes up and down Crush. "Now why the hell do you need a bodyguard?"

"I've told you about my stalker."

Adam scoffed. "Everybody here has a stalker. I have fifteen of them. Even Sterling has a stalker."

"Unfortunately, mine is a senior citizen," Sterling chimed in. "A stalker-with-a-walker, you might say."

Crush smiled at that and Sterling noticed. "Ah, an appreciative audience. I can't tell you how long it's been since I had one of those." He extended a hand that looked like it was made of rope and old wood. Crush took it and felt a strong, firm handshake. "I'm Sterling Bolsinger," the old man said, as if Crush should know the name.

It did sound vaguely familiar to Crush, but he didn't think vaguely would be enough for Sterling. "Caleb Rush," was all he said in reply.

"Where'd you serve, Caleb?"

"Iraq."

Sterling nodded. "Korea. One Marine can always recognize another."

"You don't know who he is, do you, Mr. Rush?" Adam asked.

"No, I don't. Sorry about that," Crush said to Sterling.

"But you know who *I* am?" Adam said with a grin.

"Yes." He thought to add, "I'm sorry about that, too," but decided against it.

Adam laughed. "See? I *am* more famous than you. Despite your two Oscars."

"Three," Sterling corrected him.

"One was for screenplay. Nobody counts screenplay."

Rachel spoke up. "Sterling Bolsinger is one of the greatest film directors of the sixties and seventies."

"The eighties and nineties, not so much," Sterling said modestly.

"And in the twenty-first century, he can't get arrested," Adam said. "That's what's wrong with this fucking business. These teenage executives have no sense of history. If there was any justice, I'd be bringing him coffee and wiping his ass instead of directing multimillion-dollar pictures. But such is life."

Sterling smiled at Adam and Rachel and said, "As it is, you two are nominated for Academy Awards, while I play a corrupt but lovable senator in your latest digital production."

"The lovable part is all you, Sterling," Adam said. Crush heard real fondness in his voice. Maybe Adam wasn't a total waste of space after all.

"Thank you, Adam. You plucked me from obscurity and let the world say, 'Is *that* Sterling Bolsinger? I had no idea he was still alive.'"

"They all remember you, Sterling," Adam said.

Sterling turned to Crush. "It's a sad day when the best thing anyone can say about you is 'they remember you.'"

"Most people don't get that," Crush said.

"To quote Woody Allen, 'I don't want to achieve immortality through my work; I want to achieve immortality through not dying,'" Sterling said with a crooked smile.

Rachel moved in front of Adam. "I read your latest draft of the script, Adam."

Adam held up his hand to her, palm outward. "Stop

right there. I don't talk shop at parties. If you don't want to watch the movie, I suggest you go and get some sleep. We have to be in New Orleans tomorrow for the table read."

"In this draft, I die. At the end of the first act. I don't come back."

"You're talking shop." Adam got up and started to walk away.

"Damn right, I'm talking shop," she said, blocking his path, staring him down in the rippling lights of the pool. "You gave all my good scenes to that bitch Brenda Perez."

"Brenda's a real find."

"Fuck that. I'm a real find. You found me."

"You're last year's news, Rachel."

"I got nominated for a fucking Oscar."

"That's just what I mean. Best Supporting Actress is the kiss of death in this business. When was the last time you heard anything about Marisa Tomei? Or Mira Sorvino? Or Renée fucking Zellweger?"

"That isn't why you're doing this," Rachel said. "You know why you're doing this."

"Why am I doing this? It couldn't be that it's right for the movie? It couldn't be that."

"No, it couldn't be that."

"Then what's the reason? You think it's because Brenda sucks my cock and you won't? Please. Everybody sucks my cock."

"It's because of Polly, isn't it?" Rachel said. "It's because of your girlfriend."

"Polly is a good judge of character," Adam said.

Crush sprang into action. He reacted to the warning signal even before his mind registered it. He moved by pure instinct, diving toward Adam and throwing him to the ground just as the report of the gunshot sounded and the bullet hit the concrete behind them.

He had seen the green pinpoint of light dancing on Adam's chest and knew at once what it was. A laser sight for a rifle.

Once he hit the ground, Crush threw himself over Adam, covering the smaller man's body with his. Only then did he turn and look to his Principal, the one he was supposed to be protecting. Rachel.

She was looking down at them in surprise. The green dot danced in the middle of the tattoo on her arm.

Crush launched himself at her. Fast, but too late. The gunshot sounded through the night, and Rachel twisted from the impact and fell into the pool.

CHAPTER FIVE

It was a cool night and the water felt warm as Crush jack-knifed into the pool. Adam must have kept the temper-ature as high as a Jacuzzi. Quickly, Crush swam toward Rachel's sinking body. He wrapped his arms around her and pushed off the bottom of the pool, propelling himself to the surface. She was dead weight in his arms, either un-conscious or worse.

He swam with her to the water's edge and pushed her up onto the coping. Having hoisting himself up, drip-ping wet, he bent over her, checking to see if she was still breathing. Her eyes were closed and her chest rose and fell with a steady rhythm. He sent up a silent prayer of thanks to whatever God might be looking out for her.

The wound to her arm was superficial. The bullet had just grazed the soft flesh of her deltoid muscle, right in the middle of the spiderweb tattoo. She was either in-credibly lucky that the bullet had only clipped her, or unlucky that it had touched her at all.

Once Crush knew that she was all right, he glanced up to look for the shooter. The brush-covered hillside sur-rounding them provided ample cover. If the sniper had wanted to, he could still be taking potshots at the pool. Either he had fled or he was waiting for more game. He wouldn't have to wait long. When Crush turned his head to take in the scene, he saw that all the guests were running around the house and grounds in a panic, trying to flee the scene. No one ran to Rachel's side to see how she was. They were more interested in saving their own asses.

Adam was still stretched out on the ground, looking stunned. Glancing up at the hillside, Crush saw a slender man scrambling down toward the patio, moving with a stiff-legged, awkward grace. When he moved into the light, Crush could see that it was Sterling. He moved pretty well for an old man.

Sterling hurried to Rachel's side, panting like a racehorse that had just won the Kentucky Derby. "How is she?"

"She's all right," Crush replied.

"I went after the sniper, but he took off."

"You could have been shot."

"Not a bad way to go, huh?" he said with a grin. "Picked off in the middle of a fancy Hollywood party, trying to nail a gunman? That would make a good last line for my obituary." He laughed. "Oh, my obituary is going to be *epic*."

"We've got to get her to a doctor."

"There's a doctor here." He moved off into the house, where pandemonium reigned.

Crush glanced back at Adam, who was coming to his senses, shaking his head. Adam looked over at Rachel and the small puddle of blood that was forming around her. "Oh, shit," Adam said.

Sterling walked up with a short, gnomish woman of indeterminate age and led her around the pool to where Rachel lay. "This is Dr. Alva ten Berge, the Udells' personal physician."

"That makes me sound like a Dr. Feelgood," Dr. ten

Berge said with a slight foreign accent that Crush couldn't place. "I assure you I'm anything but." The doctor bent down and examined Rachel's wound with admirable efficiency. She had short gray hair and a severe, lined face that reminded Crush of Rosa Klebb, the evil Spectre agent in *From Russia with Love*.

As Dr. ten Berge opened Rachel's eyes and examined her pupils, Adam stood up and stared down at his bleeding starlet. "She's not dead, is she?"

"No, but she's been shot," Sterling said.

"Jesus Christ. Jesus Christ. Who shot her?"

"We don't know," Sterling said. "It came from up there," he said, pointing to the hills. "Must have had a night-vision scope. Damn good shot."

Adam's gaze followed Sterling's finger to the hillside. He darted behind the table for cover and fumbled to get his cell phone out of his jeans. "I'll call 911."

"Put the phone away, Adam," Rachel said. Crush turned to see her, eyes open, lying on the concrete but looking at Adam.

"What?" Adam said.

"Put...the phone...away." Rachel sounded groggy but emphatic.

"She's right." This was another woman's voice. A voice confident and full of command, speaking up from behind them. Turning, Crush saw a tall, rangy woman in her forties with wavy brown hair and a bemused expression on her aquiline features. "Put the phone away."

"Get down," Adam warned her. "He might still be out there."

The woman didn't move an inch. "Oh please, if whoever it was wanted to shoot us, we'd all be dead by now. Put the phone back in your pants. You don't want the police piling in here, do you? And reporters?"

"Why not?" Adam asked.

"The tabloids are already lying about us," Rachel said, sitting up. "This would just give them more juice. It wouldn't be fair to Polly."

The woman shot Rachel an annoyed look. "How nice of you to care. Put the phone away, Adam."

Adam put the phone away.

So the woman was Polly, Adam's girlfriend. Any other time Crush might have been distracted by her lithe, muscular body, now he just marveled at the control she seemed to have over Adam.

Rachel touched her bleeding arm. "We can handle this on our own."

Polly turned to Dr. ten Berge. "Can you administer first aid to our Oscar nominee here?"

"Of course," the doctor said. "She's not badly hurt."

"Oh, yes," grumbled Sterling. "She's only been shot. No reason to make a big deal out of it."

While they were talking, Crush pulled off his T-shirt, tore a strip off the bottom, and started to tie it around Rachel's wound. Dr. ten Berge stopped him, saying, "That's not sanitary. We'll take her into the bedroom. Do you have a first-aid kit, Polly?"

Polly seemed distracted by Crush's bare, muscular chest and by the tattoo that covered it. A skull with a knife in its jaws in front of the onion dome of an Orthodox cathedral. The image was slightly blue and faded with time, but that only added to the eerie effect. She tore her eyes away, reluctantly, and answered the doctor's question. "In the bathroom. And use the maid's room, for God's sake. I don't want her bleeding all over my matelassé coverlet."

Crush helped Rachel get to her feet while Sterling led the way, brushing past Polly as they moved. "That's Polly, by the way," Adam said to Crush. "Polly Coburn, this is Caleb Rush."

"Hi," Polly said, with a hint of a smile. "How do you like the party so far, Mr. Rush?"

◉

The furnishings of the maid's room, when they got there, were all in white. White wallpaper, white chairs, white curtains, white pillows on a white bedspread. Rachel's blood provided a vivid contrast to the snowy landscape. Dr. ten Berge bound up Rachel's wound with gauze and an ACE bandage, which she wrapped firmly around her bicep.

"Does that feel too tight?" the doctor asked.

"A little bit," Rachel said, wincing.

"Good," Dr. ten Berge said. "That means it's tight enough."

Adam watched from the other side of the room, full of concern. Next to him stood Polly, who was smoking an e-cigarette and looking bored. "Can she go home now?" Polly asked.

"No," the doctor said.

"Honey, she's been shot," Adam said.

"Oh, it's just a scratch. Isn't it just a scratch, Alva?"

"As bullet wounds go," the doctor answered, "it's just a scratch. But it's still a bullet wound. Let her rest." She pulled a bottle of pills out of her pocket and handed them to Rachel. "You're in pain. Take one of these," she said as she got up to go.

"You take those pills with you to parties?" Crush asked

as she walked past him.

"You never know when they might be needed."

"But you're no Dr. Feelgood?"

She leveled her cold, gray eyes on Crush. "You have no idea who I am. Let's keep it that way." And she was gone. Crush felt a chill run down his spine.

"Polly, we have to let her stay. She *did* save my life, you know," Adam said.

"Please. That muscular man with the tattoos saved your life," she said. "Rachel had nothing to do with it."

"She brought him here," he said.

"Fine," Polly admitted. "She was *instrumental* in saving your life. Buy her some flowers, give her a necklace. But send her home."

"I don't have a home, Polly," Rachel said. "Not here. I live in New York."

"Then go back to your hotel."

"I got kicked out of my hotel."

"Why?" Polly asked.

"I couldn't pay my bill. I live beyond my means."

Polly rolled her eyes.

"She's staying here, Polly, that's all there is to it," Adam said, drawing himself up taller. "And another thing. I'm thinking about that rewrite of the script. I think we might have killed her off too soon."

Polly looked at Adam in dull surprise. "We'll talk about this later," she said and stalked from the room, taking time to cast a significant glance back at Crush and his ink work. "Pleased to meet you, Mr. Rush. You're quite a work of art," she said, looking at his chest.

Crush shrugged. "I had this done when I was young."

"Oh," she said, "the tattoos are nice, too."

When she shut the door behind her, Sterling spoke to

Adam from Rachel's bedside. "Someone tried to kill both of you. Am I the only one who's interested in that?"

"Shut up, old man," Adam snapped. "When I want to hear from you, I'll ask." Sterling shut up. He might be the legendary director, but it was clear who was king in this house.

"Rachel, your stalker," Adam said to Rachel. "What's his name?"

"Oh, you believe in him now?" she asked.

"Don't be a smartass. What's his name?"

"Brandon Renbourn," Crush said.

Adam looked at Crush as if he'd forgotten the big man was there. "Okay." He studied Crush for second, as if appraising him, and then said, "He needs to be taken care of."

"Taken care of?" Crush asked. "How do you mean?"

"He's a dangerous man. He tried to shoot me. He shot Rachel. He needs to be taken care of."

"By me?"

"You're her bodyguard, aren't you? You're hired to keep her safe? Fine. See to it that he doesn't try to kill her again."

"And how should I do that?"

Adam looked at him with a steady gaze. He was the movie director now. He was used to being obeyed. Crush guessed Polly was the only person who could make him tremble. "Use your discretion, Mr. Rush."

"This is a little outside my wheelhouse, Mr. Udell."

"Is it?" he asked.

Rachel laughed. "Oh, yeah," she said. "Why don't you tell him all about your wheelhouse, Crush?"

"You'll be well compensated, I assure you," Adam said. "How does ten thousand sound?"

"It sounds like you can afford it."

"Where does Renbourn live?" Adam asked Rachel.

"Hollywood. A little apartment off Franklin."

Crush looked at Rachel's wounded arm. He had a quick vision of her playing with her Pokémon cards when she was ten. He made up his mind. "It doesn't matter," he said. "Brandon's not at home. I'll be right back."

"Where are you going?" Rachel asked.

"To protect you."

As Crush walked to the door, Adam knelt by the bed and tenderly brushed Rachel's hair out of her face. "You're not going to die," he said.

She glanced at her arm. "I didn't think it was that serious."

"No. In the movie. You're not going to die in the movie."

Rachel smiled a radiant smile. "I never thought you'd kill me, Adam."

CHAPTER SIX

With a deliberate stride, Crush walked through the house, past the movie memorabilia and the sweeping circular staircase, through the confused celebrities milling about like wandering sheep without a border collie. He went to the door and glanced around, looking for Lex. He was nowhere to be seen. Crush thought he was a pretty poor excuse for a bouncer and walked into the night.

Outside it was pure chaos. Photographers were busy snapping pictures of the partygoers as they demanded their cars, overwhelming the poor parking valets who were unprepared for this sudden exodus. Elbowing his way through the horde, Crush moved to the rear of the pack, toward a portly man in a polo shirt with a big camera hanging from a strap around his neck.

Crush grabbed the camera and twisted it. The strap wrapped around the man's throat and choked him. Crush turned to a bearded paparazzo to his right and asked, "Has this guy been here all night?"

The paparazzo looked at him in surprise. "No, he just got here."

"That's what I thought," Crush said and began to lead the portly man away like a dog on a leash. "Where's your car?" he demanded.

The only reply he got was a wheezing gurgle from the

pudgy man's neck. He released the camera strap just a little and the man whispered hoarsely, "Fuck you."

Crush twirled the camera around to tighten the strap again. "Where's your car?" he repeated.

The man's eyes bugged out and he pointed to a silver RAV4 parked down the hill.

Crush loosened the strap a bit so the guy didn't die and led him to the car, gesturing with his free hand for him to unlock the door. The fat man pulled his keys out of his pocket, pressed a button, and the door locks popped up. Crush grabbed the keys from him, opened the side door, and shoved him inside. Slamming the door shut, he walked around to the driver's door and got in. The fat man could have taken that opportunity to make a run for it but Crush had bet he wouldn't. He was too busy unwrapping the camera strap from his throat and trying to breathe.

Crush started the car and slammed his foot on the accelerator. The car lurched forward and the man was thrown back against the seat. He looked less like Raymond Burr in person.

"You're Brandon Renbourn."

"Who wants to know?"

Crush slammed on the brakes. The car jerked to a halt and Brandon was propelled toward the windshield. He hadn't fastened his seat belt, so his forehead cracked against the glass.

"Brandon Renbourn?" Crush said. He hit the accelerator and tore down the road again.

"Yes, damn it," Brandon said, rubbing his head. "What do you want?"

"Are you wondering how Rachel is?"

"You mean my wife? Why doesn't she call me? Is

she okay?"

"She's not your wife."

"Well, we kept the marriage a secret. Her career and all."

"Did you take a shot at her with a rifle tonight?"

"What? No! Of course not."

"Did you take a shot at Adam Udell?"

"That sleazebag? I wish somebody would."

"Somebody did."

"Good. He's taking advantage of her. I tell her that time and again."

"When you talk to her?"

"Well, when I text her. We don't get to spend much time together. Her career and all."

"And you send her pictures?"

"Just to let her know I'm looking out for her."

"Pictures with her eyes cut out and blood painted on her face?"

"Well, see, you have to understand our relationship. That's meant in fun."

"Fun?"

"Just, 'Ha-ha, I'll gouge your eyes out.' But I wouldn't, of course. It's our way of flirting."

Crush took the twisting road at high speed, like a pro. He drove off onto the shoulder and came to a screeching stop just at the edge of a steep hillside. In front of them, the lights of Los Angeles twinkled like the stars in HD. "Flirting?" Crush asked.

"Yeah. It's our way. It's cute. Most people think I'm crazy, but Rachel, she *gets* me. We're so much alike."

"She took out a restraining order against you. You've broken it."

"Well, first of all, I haven't. I haven't been within five

hundred feet of her. And second, that was all a misunderstanding. We laughed about it during the reception."

"The reception?"

"In Vegas. After we got married."

"Just stop..."

"Look, I know you mean well. You protected her in the parking lot of that club, I appreciate that. Those photographers are such scumbags."

"You were there?"

"I'm always there."

"Just not tonight? When she was being shot?"

"Wait a minute, was she really shot? Is she okay?"

"She's okay. You only winged her."

"Winged? I should call her." He pulled his cell phone out of his pocket. Crush knocked it out of his hands.

"Look, I don't care if you shot her or not. I don't want you near her. Ever again. Do you understand?"

"That's impossible."

"Do you understand?"

"If I'm not around, who'll protect her?"

"I will. From you."

"No, no." Brandon shook his head rapidly. "How do I know you're not one of the vampires?"

"Vampires?"

"The ones who want to hurt her. Like Udell. Did he hire you? Are you working for that creep?"

"Yes, I'm working for him. He's paying me to get rid of you."

Brandon laughed. It didn't sound like a real laugh. It was more like a bad actor's laugh in a dinner theater production of some Neil Simon farce.

"You can't scare me off," Brandon said. "I'm too powerful. Being crazy makes you powerful." He reached down and pulled a large hunting knife from a sheath he had strapped to his leg. He swung it up toward Crush's throat, but not fast enough to do any damage. Crush blocked it with his left forearm and wrenched Brandon's wrist with his right hand until he heard a satisfying crack. Brandon dropped the knife.

"Ow!" Brandon said.

Crush calmly moved his face close to Brandon's, his blue eyes staring deeply into the pudgy man's brown ones. "You think *you're* crazy? You don't *know* crazy."

Crush floored it. The RAV4 sped toward the edge of the bluff and Crush opened the door and jumped out. Brandon just had time to leap from the car before it zoomed off the cliff and plunged down the steep escarpment.

Brandon hit the dirt and rolled over and over. His skin was torn from his hands as he tried to grab at the gravel and stop himself. Finally his left leg twisted under him and served as a brake. He lay still, panting and moaning. He cradled his wrist to his chest, and his left leg was turned at an ugly angle. Crush stood over him as he looked up, blood dripping into his eyes from the cut in his scalp.

"My car!" he said. "You wrecked my car!"

"If I ever see you again, I'll kill you," Crush said quietly. Then he started walking down the road back to Adam's house.

"Where are you going? You can't leave me here!" Brandon cried out. "At least lend me your phone. Let me call an Uber!"

Crush didn't answer. This wasn't quite his wheelhouse, he thought, but he'd always been good at improvising.

◉

The street was quiet when Crush finally made it all the way back to the villa. It was after four in the morning and the guests, the valets, and even the paparazzi had gone. It seemed hushed and peaceful, but Crush could make out the sounds of the night that are usually drowned out by human activity: tree frogs singing from the branches, owls hooting in the treetops, raccoons or rats scuffling in the underbrush, and, in the distance, coyotes yipping like maniacs. It reminded him that, even without people, the night was filled with dangers.

He walked to the front door, noticed that it was slightly ajar, pushed it open, and stepped inside. In the darkened room, he could just make out Sterling, his lanky form sprawled on the circular staircase. He had a cigarette in one hand and a glass of bourbon in the other.

"I wondered when you'd get back," he said, raising the glass in a toast. "Come on in and shut the door." The old man got up and walked through the sliding doors to the pool. Crush did as he was told and started to follow Sterling, but then took a detour to the maid's room. Peeking in, he saw Rachel sleeping peacefully. Adam Udell sat in a chair by the bed. He was still fully dressed, his head was slumped forward on his chest, and he snored fitfully. He looked like a worried parent at his child's hospital bed. Crush shut the door quietly. He hated to admit it, but Adam seemed almost human in there.

As he turned, he saw Polly standing in the hall. "Is he fucking her?"

"No," Crush said.

She nodded as if her worst suspicions had been confirmed and then turned and walked away. She was wearing a bathrobe that clung to her hips provocatively as she moved down the hallway. Crush wondered whom she intended to provoke.

Sterling was sitting at a table out by the pool. He smiled as Crush came out to join him. "Ah, there you are. Join me in a drink?"

Crush sat across from him. "No thanks."

"I see." Sterling raised his bushy eyebrows. "Are you a friend of Bill's?" he asked, using the old-fashioned AA slang for alcoholic.

Crush nodded.

"I used to be an alcoholic," Sterling said, taking a sip of bourbon. "Now I'm a drunk. It's much simpler." He took a drag of a cigarette. "How long have you been sober?"

"This time? Two years."

Sterling nodded. "I was sober for twenty years. Quit smoking for thirty."

"What changed?"

"I wanted to live longer. Now I've lived long enough." He looked down at the bourbon in his glass. "Adam only stocks the most expensive bourbon. Hirsch Reserve. A grand a bottle." He took another sip and made a face. "Give me Old Crow any day. Oh well, beggars can't be choosers."

"I don't know about that," Crush said. "Beggars can be the most demanding people I know."

Sterling laughed his silent laugh again. "Very true, Crush."

Crush was surprised to hear Sterling call him by his street name. "Have you known Rachel long?" he asked.

"Long enough to know her as Rachel Fury," Sterling said. "Before she was rechristened as Strayhorn."

"Did you introduce her to Adam?" Crush asked.

"That I did. You might say that the little minx used

me," he chuckled. "But only after I encouraged her. Just needed a little nudge. She has talent, that one."

"For what?"

"Acting. What did you think I meant?" Sterling sounded a little offended. Rachel had a lot of protectors here.

"That's what I thought you meant," Crush said.

"Hmmm. She says you're a good friend." He sounded dubious. "She needs friends."

"I know." Crush only wished she knew that.

"Did you see to that stalker?" Sterling asked.

"Yep."

"You didn't kill him, did you?"

"No."

"That's good." Sterling looked into his glass as if it held an answer to the question he was about to ask. "Do you think he's the one who fired those shots tonight?"

"Do you?"

"I don't think so. From what Rachel tells me, Brandon's more of a knife man."

"You may be right."

"Still, better safe than sorry."

"That's what I thought."

"But what if Brandon wasn't the shooter?"

"All right, what then?"

"That would mean the shooter's still out there." Sterling's eyes glittered as he spoke, like he'd just come up with a new twist on an old story. "And you know what else that could mean?"

"Not really."

Sterling looked frustrated that Crush wasn't following his lead. "Rachel tells me she only hired you to look after her tonight."

"That's right. She's going to New Orleans tomorrow. Or today, I guess. That's outside my jurisdiction."

Sterling leaned forward, sliding a business card across the table. "How would you like to make some real money, Mr. Rush?"

Crush picked it up and looked at it. It was a simple card of heavy gray chipboard, embossed with the words: STERLING BOLSINGER: STORYTELLER. *Nice*, he thought, slipping the card into his jeans. "Sorry, I already have a job."

Sterling smiled. "Do you know who was president when I was born? Franklin Delano Roosevelt. FDR. That makes me history, Mr. Rush. That makes me a fucking dinosaur. I've seen so many people born and die, I feel like God Almighty. But you know what I've never seen? I've never seen a man who had what he wanted. What do you want, Mr. Rush?"

Crush thought it over. "I haven't figured that out yet."

"A wise answer. I didn't find out I didn't know what I wanted until I was sixty-five. Most people think they know, but when they get it, they're disappointed. Be it a woman, or a fortune, or..."

"An Oscar?"

"Yes, especially that."

"Rachel doesn't particularly want the Oscar."

"I know that. But Adam does. He wants an Academy Award like Fred C. Dobbs wanted the treasure of the Sierra Madre."

The bourbon sloshing around in Sterling's glass was looking awfully good to Crush. "Do you like Adam Udell?" he said, changing the subject.

"Oh, I don't suppose anybody *likes* Adam. But I care for him like a son. A prodigal son, but a son nonetheless.

That's why I want you to keep working for Rachel. To go with her to New Orleans."

Crush looked at him blankly.

"Don't be so damned elaborate, Sterling." Crush was startled to hear Polly speaking right behind him. "Just ask him."

"Polly, I'm going at this in my own way," Sterling grumbled.

Polly pulled up a chair and sat a little too close to Crush. "It's very simple. Adam won't hire a bodyguard. He thinks they're not manly or some such nonsense. We want you to protect Adam while it *looks* like you're protecting Rachel."

"What makes you think Adam needs protecting?"

Polly looked at Crush like he was a special-needs child. "Oh now, you don't really think that shooter was aiming for Rachel, do you?"

CHAPTER SEVEN

A gust of wind blew up from the hillside and fluttered the fringes of Sterling's gray hair and the hem of Polly's bathrobe. Crush could make out the outline of her breasts in the moonlight. He brought his mind back to the subject at hand. "You think Adam was the target?"

"Yes," she said.

"Then why take the second shot at Rachel?"

"He was still aiming for Adam. She just got in the way."

"Do you have any idea who the shooter was?"

Polly shrugged. "It doesn't matter."

"What matters is who was behind it," Sterling said. "Have you ever heard of Meier Lustig?"

Crush had heard of him. Meier Lustig was the leader of the Israeli Mafia on the West Coast. He was responsible for half the drug trafficking, extortion, embezzlement, and money laundering in Los Angeles, not to mention a number of murders.

"How did Adam get mixed up with Lustig?"

Sterling sat forward on the edge of his chair. "There's a thing that happens when you become a motion picture director. A successful one, at any rate. While you're on top, you're the chief. The top dog. The lord of the manor. You get whatever you want. Everyone says 'yes' to you, all day long. Crew members, actors, maître d's, movie stars, studio executives...they all do precisely what you want, whenever you want it. You come to think you're invincible. It gets to be second nature. Predictable. Boring, even. So you start looking for equals. Not other directors; they're competition. Other rich people. Politicians. Inventors. Captains of industry."

"Mob bosses?"

Sterling nodded. "That's how deluded you can get. You actually believe you hold the power of life and death over other people. You forget it's just pretend. You think you're on par with someone who has people killed as a matter of course. You think it's fun to hang out with them. To party with them. You love to hear their war stories. And they love to hear yours as well. Because everybody, even Meier Lustig himself, wants to be a motion picture director."

"Are we talking about Adam Udell or you?" Crush asked.

"We're talking about every goddamned, asshole A-list movie director who ever lived."

"Sterling exaggerates," Polly said. "Not every A-list movie director is an asshole."

"Name one who isn't," Sterling said.

"Ron Howard," she said.

"All right, there's always the exception that proves the rule," he said. "I spent some time in Lustig's orbit myself, in my asshole days. But even at the height of my assholeness, I was never dumb enough to screw Meier Lustig's mistress and think I could get away with it."

"You see," Polly said, "Meier wanted Adam to give his mistress a part in his last movie. Adam was only too happy to agree. Unfortunately, Adam started to think of her as a fuckable cast member instead of the property of the most dangerous man on the West Coast."

"Or a woman in her own right?"

"Why, Mr. Rush, I'd never have pegged you for a feminist," Polly said.

"I'm full of surprises," Crush said. "So Meier found out about it?"

"We assume so," Sterling said. "Anyway, Kristin Quinn—that was the poor girl's name—was one of those Valley rats who spent her whole life dreaming of making it big without ever knowing how or why. She was thrilled to have a real part in a real movie, but on the day her scene was supposed to be shot—well, her two lines anyway—she didn't show up. We waited. There was no word from her. Nothing. She hasn't been heard from since. That was six months ago."

"So you think Lustig killed her?"

"Could be."

"That's terrible."

"I know," Polly said, "we had to re-cast the role and everything."

"But why would Lustig be going after Adam?"

"Jealousy has a huge appetite."

"But why would he wait until now to strike back?" Crush asked.

"To make Adam squirm. Lustig has a bizarre sense of humor about these things."

"But you don't really know, do you? That it was Lustig?"

"Two days ago, we received this in the mail. From Lustig." Polly pulled an envelope from the pocket of her bathrobe and handed it to Crush.

"How do you know it's from Lustig?"

"It has his return address on it."

"What's in it?"

She took it from him and opened it. Inside was a pressed flower. "It's a purple rose. Adam has a ridiculous habit of sending a bouquet of them to all his conquests," she explained. "At least until he's tired of them."

"How many conquests has he made this year?"

"Seven. No, eight. Eight worthy of roses."

"That's seven other possibilities."

She drew a few strands of yellow hair from the envelope. "But only one was a blonde. My boyfriend usually prefers brunettes." Crush couldn't help but notice that Polly was a brunette. Rachel, on the other hand, was a redhead, dyed at the moment platinum blond.

"What do you expect me to do about it? Why don't you go to the police?"

"And really piss Meier off? Not a chance. You just need to keep Adam alive until we settle this," Polly said.

"And how are you planning on settling it?"

"I'll talk to him," said Polly. "I handle all of Adam's difficult negotiations."

"If what you're telling me is true, you're dealing with a sociopath who thinks he's been wronged. You might find yourself a little out of your league."

"Please," she said. "I've gone toe-to-toe with Harvey Weinstein. I think I can handle a hoodlum from Tel Aviv."

"And if you can't?"

"I've never come across any deal I couldn't close," she said.

Ordinarily, Crush would have thought anyone who would say that about Meier Lustig was thoroughly deluded. However, looking at Polly's determined gaze, he was half convinced that she could pull it off.

"Well, I wish you luck," Crush said, pushing back from the table. "But I'm going to have to decline."

"If it's a matter of money…" Polly began.

"It's a funny thing about money," Crush said. "You always need just a little bit more than what you have. Well, I got off that train a long time ago. Now I just want what I need. No more, no less. You should try it sometime."

He walked back through the sliding glass doors into the house, thinking that those were good parting words. Then it occurred to him that he didn't have a ride home. He didn't know if Uber was still functioning in these parts past four-thirty in the morning, but he couldn't very well stop and check now. It would spoil his exit.

"Don't want to wait and say goodbye to Rachel?" Sterling called after him.

"We run into each other every two or three years," Crush said. "I'll say goodbye to her then."

It was nearly seven in the morning when the Lyft car dropped Crush off in front of the American Cement Building on Wilshire Boulevard at MacArthur Park. He walked in and rode the elevator to the fifth floor. The sun was just rising over the Westlake Theatre sign as he opened the door to his loft and kicked off his shoes.

K.C. Zerbe, Crush's sort-of brother, who was padding around in his slippers, Frankenstein boxers, and Green Lantern T-shirt, looked up as he walked in. "Why didn't you call? I was worried sick."

"Really?"

"No, but I was bored. We could have at least played Words with Friends."

"You always beat me."

"I have a lot of time to practice," Zerbe said. "You

want some breakfast?"

"What have you got?"

"Well, you haven't been to the market since Wednesday, so I could make you oatmeal or a kale and spinach omelet."

"Oatmeal."

"You always say oatmeal."

Zerbe busied himself at the stove while Crush changed into his sweats. Having breakfast before going to bed at seven in the morning wasn't too unusual for him. A routine schedule was not a part of Caleb Rush's lifestyle.

He walked into the main room and plopped onto the sofa, a well-thumbed copy of Marcus Aurelius's *Meditations* in his big hands.

"Why do you always read that?" Zerbe asked.

"It's cool."

"Really?"

"Marcus Aurelius was a Roman emperor and philosopher. He wrote this book of meditations while he was leading the imperial army against the Germanic tribes. Whenever anyone says somebody is cool, I always think, yeah, but is he 'leading an imperial army against the Germanic tribes while writing a classic book of stoic philosophy' cool?"

"That's pretty cool. What does Marcus have to say today?"

"How ridiculous he is who is surprised at anything which happens in this life," Crush read aloud.

"Groovy," Zerbe said. "Breakfast is served."

Over a hot bowl of rolled oats, Crush told the story of his evening. He only covered the highlights, but it still took about fifteen minutes.

"Interesting," Zerbe said. "All I did was rob a bunch of

casinos in Las Vegas."

"You watched *Ocean's Eleven* again?"

"Both versions. I like the new one better, but the old one has Sammy Davis Jr. in it. I wish there was a way to put Sammy Davis Jr. in the new one. Then it would be perfect."

"With modern technology, anything is possible." Crush ate another spoonful of oatmeal. "How are your mad computer skills?"

"Pretty mad."

"Could you keep an eye out for Brandon Renbourn's whereabouts?"

"How do you mean?"

"Just see if he shows up on any databases or anything."

"You have no idea how computers work, do you?"

"Not really."

"I'll see what I can do."

They were silent for a moment. The sound of morning rush hour traffic from Wilshire Boulevard drifted up to them. "So you're not going?" Zerbe asked.

"Going where?"

"To New Orleans. To protect Rachel?"

"They don't want me to protect Rachel. They want me to protect Udell."

"You could do both."

"She doesn't need protecting. She can take care of herself."

"But what if she gets in the way of another stray bullet?"

"That won't happen."

"Maybe not," Zerbe said. "Unless..."

Crush shot Zerbe an irritated glance. "Unless what?"

"Unless Lustig's man *was* aiming for her. You know,

'You took my woman, I'll take yours.' "

"You watch too much Turner Classic Movies."

"It's my window on the world."

"Rachel will be fine. Trust me."

"Okay. She'll be staying in a hotel?"

"I suppose."

"You could take that toy I made. See if it works on the doors."

"What toy?"

"The dry-erase marker with the special modifications."

"You'll have to try it out on your own. I'm not going."

Zerbe nodded. He took the book from Crush and flipped through it. He found a passage and read it. *"Everything—a horse, a vine—is created for some duty... For what task, then, were you yourself created?"*

Crush made a face. He got up and went to his room, picking up his jeans from where he'd tossed them and digging into the back pocket. He pulled out Sterling's business card and entered his number into his cell phone.

"Hello," Sterling answered, sounding like he'd been pulled from a deep sleep. "Who is this?"

"Crush. What time are we leaving for New Orleans?"

◉

Crush met Rachel at Van Nuys Airport, where she was supposed to join Adam, Polly, and Sterling on Adam's private jet. He'd never flown on a private jet before. When he was working for Tigon Security, his range was strictly Los Angeles and LA adjacent. Crush hated to fly. He hated the cramped seats. He hated the security lines. He hated giving up his freedom for a quicker trip between two places. Oh, and he hated going up in the air and possibly crashing in a fiery ball of flame.

But all those problems, except the last one, were nonexistent in Adam Udell's world. No lines, no TSA agents rudely frisking him, no worries about being crammed into a tiny seat next to a crying baby.

Crush drove up to the private airfield, parked his car, and walked into a place that looked like the VIP room in a fancy nightclub. Only the passengers for that flight were gathered on sofas in the lounge, drinking cocktails and waiting for Adam to show up. Just Rachel, Polly, Sterling, and a new face, Byron Douglas, the male lead of *The Rage Machine* and *The Rage Machine II: The Redemption*, as the current movie was called.

Byron had been known for years as the dull-but-lovable veterinarian dad on the sitcom *Family Practice*. He had recently re-invented himself as the unbelievably muscular Enforcer, the Rage Machine—a genetically created, existentially lonely brute from the twenty-third century who "learns to love." Crush knew this because he had Zerbe look up the movie on IMDB. What the Enforcer learns in the sequel, Crush couldn't guess.

As he stood up to greet Crush, Byron looked more like the befuddled dad from TV than the killer of the movie, though he was now so bulked up, his muscles strained against his carefully selected, too small T-shirt. He almost made Crush look puny by comparison. Almost.

"So you're Crush!" Byron said. "Awesome. Rachel's told me all about you!"

When Byron shook his hand, Crush looked down at his wrist. It was a slight wrist, like a teenager's. From that, his arm ballooned out with rippling muscles and bulging veins, like a Popeye cartoon. However Byron had transformed himself from weakling to strongman, it hadn't been solely through hours at the gym.

"Don't believe everything you hear," Crush said.

"Listen to him! He's big and he's modest!" Byron said, laughing. Everything Byron said had an exclamation mark after it.

He slapped Crush on the back, and then he rubbed Crush's shoulders for a long second. "Whoa! You are a monster, aren't you? How long have you been this big?"

"The last couple of weeks."

"You're kidding, right? You kid! You've probably been this way your whole life! I've only been like this for a couple of years! I still look in the mirror and say, 'Whoa! Who the heck is that?' We gotta talk!"

Crush imagined that they would. Whether he wanted to or not.

Adam Udell, the Great Director, showed up half an hour after they were due to depart. It didn't seem to matter. They just walked onto the plane like they were walking into a waiting limousine and got buckled in.

The inside of the Gulfstream G550 was all polished wood and swivel seats. There was room to get up and walk around, and there were places for Crush to put his long legs. It was almost heaven. Except for the flying part. That was still terrifying. When they took off, he felt his stomach ride up to his throat. He recalled half-remembered prayers from his childhood until the plane leveled off and they achieved cruising altitude. Or, as he thought of it, collision-with-another-airplane altitude. Or collision-with-a-flock-of-birds altitude. Or engine-failure altitude. Crush's imagination was rife with possibilities.

A bone-thin flight attendant walked through the cabin serving chilled martinis and Moscow Mules. So not only did Crush have to worry about crashing, he had to worry about losing his abstinence. Those tall, cool glasses and bedewed copper mugs looked so delicious and so soothing that he almost grabbed them both and tossed them back to calm his nerves. He looked around and saw no one who could help him in his hour of need.

He turned to Rachel as a last resort. But Rachel was chugging a Moscow Mule like it was a cold lemonade on a hot day. He thought about calling his AA sponsor and pulled out his cell phone. "Can I use this?" he asked Sterling.

"I really don't know," he said. "Supposedly it interferes with the communication in the cockpit. I always thought that was just bullshit. But I've never tried it. Every time I start to dial I think...what if I bring the plane down? Just doesn't seem worth it. You can try it if you want, though."

Not worth it, Crush decided. He put the phone away and asked the flight attendant for a cranberry juice. He sipped the sour beverage and thought about what to do next. He really wanted to talk with Rachel. He hadn't been alone with her since the shooting, and he had something he wanted to clear up. But he couldn't do it with everyone around. He wanted to talk with Polly and Sterling, too, but he couldn't do that with Adam around. The only one he could talk to was Adam, and Adam was the one he was least interested in.

He walked over to look out the window over the wing. Byron maneuvered his bulky body next to Crush to look out, too. "I never get used to riding in these things!" he said. "God, I love being rich!" He turned to Crush. "Are you rich?"

"No, I'm not."

"I feel for you. I used to not be rich. Trust me, being rich is better!"

"Is it?"

"Sure. You know why? You don't have to worry about running out of money. Other than that, it's some good, some bad. But that not worrying about money thing? That's the best!"

"I'll take your word for it."

"Hey, can I ask you a question?" He took Crush by the arm and sat with him in the two free chairs by the bathroom. "Do you find that women are threatened by your body?"

"I'm not sure I understand."

"Well, when I first started bulking up, I thought my wife would love it. I mean, I'd love it if *she* got in great shape, right? But no! She just started to feel bad. Like she was 'less than,' you know? It made her feel old. And then she started thinking other women would be attracted to me."

"And were they?"

"Sure," he said. "But then, I was a star. And a star in great shape. And rich, too. So I didn't let them fool me. I knew why they wanted me. They wanted to sleep with a rich, in-shape star!"

"So you didn't sleep with them?"

"Oh, I slept with them. Lots of them! But that was after my wife left me. For my agent. Who's rich but fat. And not a star. Do you think I got to be just too much for her to handle?"

"Maybe," Crush said. "Or maybe you're just an asshole."

"You think?"

"Or maybe she is. Or maybe you both are."

Byron laughed. "I think it's that last one. We always

had a lot in common." More seriously, he said, "Can I see your abs?"

"I don't think so."

"I get the feeling you don't work at it, am I right?"

"I work out."

"Yeah, but it's not your whole life. You don't eat, sleep, and dream it. It's not your job!"

"It's not."

"But me, I *have* to be in this kind of shape! My torso is going to be digitally projected on a screen seventy feet wide. People are going to be judging me!"

"Maybe they'll be paying attention to your acting."

"Bullshit! Come on, show me."

Crush lifted up his shirt.

"I knew it!" Byron said. "You're not ripped. You're just strong!"

Crush lowered his shirt.

"The people," Byron said, "they want to see every muscle defined! That's not what a real enforcer would look like! A real enforcer would look like you!"

"I'm not an enforcer."

"But you know what I mean! It's so fake!"

"It's a movie, right. Isn't it supposed to be fake?"

He laughed. "Right! But why does it have to hurt so much to be fake?" He slapped his own belly. "What do you do? To keep in shape?"

"I work out. I eat right."

"Sure, sure." Byron leaned and whispered in his ear. "But what do you *do*?"

"I'm not sure I know what you mean."

Byron looked at him, blankly. "Are you saying God gave you that body?"

"I'm saying it's in my DNA. You should've seen my

father."

Byron sat back and shook his head. "It's just not fair. Some people have all the luck. Like them." He shot a look at Adam and Rachel. "Nominated for Oscars. All I've been nominated for is an Emmy. Emmys are so second rate." He dropped his voice to a whisper. "I hope they don't win. I'd hate to see that."

"No one says you have to watch."

"But I'm going to be there for the ceremony next week. I'm a presenter."

"Well, that's an honor."

"For Best Documentary Short Subject. That's where they stick the has-beens."

Crush clucked sympathetically and then moved back to his previous seat. Adam Udell appeared to be asleep, so he thought he'd chance it. As soon as he was settled back into the creamy leather of the chair, Adam's eyes opened. "Caleb Rush," he said.

"That's me."

"I've done some checking up on you."

"Really?" *There'd be no peace on this flight,* Crush thought. For the first time he missed being anonymously mistreated on an economy flight.

"Yes. You were with Tigon Security. You still have your guard card?" he asked, referring to the license from the California Bureau of Security and Investigative Services that all bodyguards have to carry.

"Sure."

"And you were in the Marines. In Afghanistan?"

"Iraq, but close. Nobody really knows the difference."

"I've thought of making a movie about Afghanistan. Like the old movies. Like *Gunga Din* with Cary Grant."

"Funny, it was *just* like that. Nobody gets that right."

"You're making fun of me."

"Little bit."

"People don't usually do that. I demand loyalty in the people who work for me. Above all else."

"I'm not working for you."

"You're part of my team."

"And there's no 'me' in 'team.' No wait, there is."

"Get all your wisecracks out of your system now," said Adam. "Don't joke with me on the set. On the set, I'm God."

"Really? How does God feel about that?"

"He does what I say."

"I'm here to protect Rachel. Unless you try to hurt her, I'll play along."

"I'm the director. I may have to hurt her. A little. For the good of the picture."

Crush leaned forward in his seat. "If you or anyone else does anything to harm her, I'll take you out."

Adam smiled, as if Crush had just passed a test. "I like you, Crush. You speak your mind. Most people are so fucking intimidated by me."

"Most people want something from you."

"And you don't?"

"No."

"Come on," Adam said. "If I told you I want to hire you to write a screenplay based on your life? You wouldn't jump at that?"

"Sounds like a lot of work."

"And if I wanted to give you a part in my movie?"

"Too much sitting around and waiting."

Adam laughed. "Can I say that I think you're too good to be true, Crush? Everybody has a price."

"Oh, I have a price. You just don't have what I'm

interested in."

"What are you interested in?"

"None of your business."

"I'll figure it out. If there's one thing I know, it's people."

"If you say so."

"How do you think I got to be a movie director?"

"You're a power-hungry, self-deluded psychopath?"

"All right. But I'm a power-hungry, self-deluded psychopath who knows people. And I'll figure out what your price is, Crush."

"Let me know when you do."

"Oh, I will. You can count on it."

ROYAL STREET

CHAPTER EIGHT

They landed at Louis Armstrong International and tax-ied to a private runway, where they walked down a set of stairs onto the tarmac and into a waiting stretch limo, all black with tinted windows, like they were the president or the Beatles or something. If they wanted to make a target of themselves, Crush thought, they couldn't have done it better if they'd painted red circles on their foreheads.

It was sixty degrees, which was warm for New Orleans in February, but it felt cold to Crush, being used to, as he was, LA winters. They drove into the city, traveling through the parishes to the French Quarter. Adam turned to Polly and asked if she remembered to set the alarm at the house.

She checked her cell phone. "See? It's on." She showed him a display on the phone.

"He's paranoid that someone might steal his trea-sures," she explained to Crush.

"I'm not paranoid. It has happened. Three years ago I had a very valuable item stolen from my home. It was never recovered."

"What was it?" asked Crush.

"I wouldn't expect you to understand the significance of it," Adam said.

"Try me."

"Some props from *Casablanca*. They were irreplaceable."

"That's too bad."

"Thank you for your concern." Suddenly Adam was all business.

"Now, I want you all to get some sleep tonight. We get together at ten in my suite for the table read."

"I'll be there, Chief," said Byron.

"Count me in," said Rachel.

"By the way, Rachel," Adam said, "we're going back to the last draft."

"The one where I don't die?"

"That's the one."

Rachel turned to Polly. "You okay with that, Polly?"

"He's the director," Polly said. "I'm just the editor."

"Oh, everybody knows you're much more than that," Rachel said. "You're his sounding board. You're his conscience. You're his Jiminy Cricket. He doesn't make a move without you."

"You read too many blogs," Adam said.

"So that isn't true?" she asked Polly. "You're not the power behind the throne?"

"I'm just his editor," Polly said through clenched teeth.

"Well, I appreciate it anyway."

"I didn't do it for you, Rachel," Adam said. "I did it for the good of the picture."

"Of course," Rachel said.

Polly glared at Rachel. Adam stared out the window. Rachel closed her eyes to sleep. Crush and Sterling and Byron tried not to look at anyone. The atmosphere was so thick you could cut it with a box cutter.

Their hotel was on Royal Street. The Louisiane. One

of the oldest hotels in the Vieux Carré. The production company had booked the entire tenth floor, and Adam had the William Faulkner Suite. Polly had the Tennessee Williams Suite on the right, Rachel had the Truman Capote on the left, Byron had the Ernest Hemingway next to Polly, and Sterling had the Thomas Wolfe. All those great writers had supposedly lived and worked and drank and loved there. It was a very literary establishment.

Once Crush had shut the door to the Capote Suite and he and Rachel were alone in the opulent French Creole surroundings, he took off his leather jacket and she started going through the minibar. "You'll sleep out here, Crush," she said. "I'll take the bedroom."

"Okay. Why were you goading Polly so much?"

Rachel shrugged. "She can take it."

"Sure. But you don't want to overplay your hand. She's a powerful adversary."

"This isn't *Game of Thrones*, Crush."

"Isn't it? You did what you set out to do. Adam feels protective of you. Time to pull back."

"You make it sound like I planned this."

"Let me see your cell phone."

"Why?"

"Just give it to me."

She shrugged and handed it over. Scrolling through the recent texts, he spotted the last one, sent at 1:26 yesterday morning, just about the time they'd pulled up to Adam Udell's house. It was addressed to 'D' and the message read 'IAH.'

He sighed. He hadn't wanted to find that. "Is that a code?" he asked her.

"Use your big brain."

"It could just stand for 'I am here.' "

"That's a little obvious."

"Who's D?"

"She's my life coach. I like to keep her informed as to my whereabouts."

Crush scrolled through her contacts and pressed a number. It rang a few times, and Rachel's father answered, "Hey."

"Hey, Lloyd. It's me, Crush."

"Caleb Rush! How long has it been? Could you put my daughter on?"

"I'm afraid not. The wound was more serious than we thought. She's in the hospital."

"Come off it, I only winged her."

"He's fishing, Dad," Rachel said loudly.

"Fuck you very much, Crush," said her dad.

"Where are you, Lloyd?"

"I'm just down the street," he said. "Café Lafitte. You can't miss it. It's right next to the police station. Come by. Have a cup of coffee and a beignet. It'll be my treat."

"That'll be the day." Crush ended the call and turned to Rachel. "So you relied on ol' Papa, did you?"

"Who else was I going to have do it? Dad's a crack shot." She held her arm out. The bandage covered her spider's web tattoo in the exact center. "Look, a bull's-eye."

Crush shook his head. "Why, Rachel?"

"Adam was going to kill me off! I had to do something."

"Jesus. It's a movie."

"Well, it all worked out."

"I almost killed your stalker."

"Collateral damage," she said. "Besides, it would've been no great loss. He's as crazy as the day is long."

"You're a piece of work, you know that?"

"Thank you. Look, why don't we go talk to my dad?

He'll explain everything."

"What's to explain? I really thought you were in danger, Rachel."

"I am."

"Whatever you're doing, it won't work on me."

"Let's talk to my dad. He'd love to see you."

Crush sighed. He wasn't sure the feeling was mutual.

"Let me tell Adam," she said, going to a door next to the TV and opening it, revealing another door.

"You have adjoining rooms?"

"I like to keep his hopes up." She knocked on the door. "Hey Adam, I'm going out for a beignet. Want one?"

The door flew open and a man in a ski mask burst in on them, grabbing for Rachel with black-gloved hands. Crush stepped in front of her and punched at the man's throat. He gasped and fell back into the adjoining room.

Crush stepped through the doorway as the man scrambled up and back to the writing desk. He grabbed a chair and brandished it in front of him, just as Adam came out of the bathroom, wearing a bathrobe and drying his hair.

"What the what?" said Adam.

The man threw the chair at Crush and bolted for the door. Crush dodged the flying chair and ran out after him. The man was racing down the hall to the stairway exit and Crush followed him, his feet thudding on the plush carpet. He'd nearly caught up to him when a maid, pushing a housekeeping cart, came out of a door in front of him and he collided with it. Bouncing off the cart, Crush crashed against the wall, righted himself, and kept on running.

The intruder was nowhere to be seen. Crush grabbed for the stairway door and flung it open. He heard footsteps echoing in the stairwell. Racing down the stairs, he tried to catch up with the footsteps. Down and down he ran until the footsteps stopped ringing. He stopped then too, breathing heavily and listening intently. No sound. He was on the sixth floor. The man couldn't have been more than two stories ahead of him. So he must have exited on the fifth or fourth floors.

Running down to the fifth floor, he opened the door. The hallway was empty. He ran down to the fourth floor—same thing. He thought of calling 911 and realized his cell phone was in his jacket in Rachel's room.

He went to the elevator, took it to the tenth floor, and went to the Faulkner Suite, where Adam, Rachel, and Polly were gathered. Adam was still in a Hotel Louisiane bathrobe.

"Did you get him?" Adam asked.

Crush shook his head.

"Who was he?" Polly asked. "Was he her stalker?"

"No," Crush said. "Did you call the police?"

Adam looked to Polly. Polly looked to Adam. "We thought it best not to," Adam said.

"And why was that?" Crush asked.

"They're not sure he was after me," Rachel said.

"He grabbed for your throat."

"But he was in Adam's room," Polly said. "We have to consider..."

"That Adam was the target?"

"We don't want any undue publicity," Polly said.

"And what if he killed somebody? That would be 'due publicity'?"

"Well, he didn't put up much of a fight, after all," Adam said. "You scared him and he ran. He's probably pissing his pants right now."

"Could be," Crush said. "Or he could be planning his next attack."

"Then I'm glad you're here to stop him," Polly said.

◉

It was dark and threatening rain when Crush and Rachel walked down the narrow sidewalks of the French Quarter and reached the Café Lafitte. She'd decided to keep the appointment with her father.

Lloyd Fury sat in the side courtyard at a wrought iron table, sipping from a cup of chicory-laced café au lait and eating a beignet. With his slicked jet-black hair and his pencil-thin mustache, he looked like a lothario in a 1930s movie. Powdered sugar was scattered on his shirt as if someone had loaded a shotgun full of snow and set it off in his face.

A couple of stray cats wound about the table legs and pranced over to a bowl of cat food in front of the imposing edifice of the New Orleans Police Department, right next to them. The sight of Lloyd Fury so close to, but not being booked into, a police station was something Crush never thought he'd see.

Lloyd smiled as they walked up to the table. Rachel pulled up a chair and said, "Hi, Pop."

"Hi, sugar," Lloyd replied before he turned to Crush. "Whoa, Crush, you're even bigger than I remembered. How long has it been anyway?"

"You shot your daughter," Crush said.

"What, you're getting right down to business? No preliminaries? You gotta grease the wheels, son. Ease into it. How you been? Whatcha been up to?"

"Pulling your daughter out of a swimming pool. After

you shot her."

Lloyd chuckled and his glass left eye glinted. "At least have something to eat. Try the beignets. They're to die for."

"I don't think he's hungry, Dad," she said.

"How's your arm, sweetheart?" Lloyd asked her.

"It aches," she said. "There was a doctor there. She gave me some pain pills."

"Let's see," he said. She fished a plastic bottle out of her pants and handed it over. "Demerol. I wish she'd given you hydrocodone, but beggars can't be choosers." He opened the bottle, shook a couple of pills out, popped them in his mouth, and washed them down with his café au lait. "There. That'll take the edge off."

Rachel told Lloyd about the attacker in the hotel and how Crush had chased him off.

"Whoa," Lloyd said. "Good thing Crush was there."

"Was it you?" Crush asked.

Lloyd chuckled. "I'm not as fast as I used to be. I'd have passed out before I made it to the stairs."

"And you don't know anything about it?"

"Not a thing."

"Good. I'm going," Crush said, turning on his heel.

"Wait," Lloyd said, "not so fast. Talk to me. This is a family reunion. Of a sort."

"Okay." Crush pulled up a chair. "But you did shoot Rachel by the pool, didn't you?"

"That I did," Lloyd said. "How did you know?"

"I didn't at first. I was caught up in the drama of it, like everybody else. But then I started thinking...it was just so damned convenient."

Lloyd cackled. "Convenient! Ha! I said you made the right choice, Rach! Crush is even smarter than he was at nineteen."

"Is that why you picked me for this?" Crush asked Rachel. "Because I'm smart?"

"That and other things," she said.

"There's something I want you to get straight," Crush said. "I'm not in the game anymore. I haven't pulled a con for ten years."

"I gotta say, I resent you using the word 'con,' son. It's a way of life with us."

"I know."

"The Travelers live by different rules, Crush."

Lloyd claimed that his family was descended from the Irish Travelers, a clan of gypsy-like wanderers who supposedly lived off cons, grifts, swindles, and other illegal activities. Crush had no idea if the Furys were really Travelers. He didn't even know if Travelers were actually criminals or just another misunderstood minority. But he did know that Lloyd was a charming, inveterate liar.

"I'm not a Traveler," Crush said.

"No, but you're half Russian and half dago. You know how important blood is."

"My blood's no different from anybody else's."

Lloyd chuckled. "Look at him, Rach. Half Cossack and half Roman centurion and he tells me bloodlines don't matter. We Travelers can trace our line back to the time of Christ. When Our Lord was being crucified, one of our ancestors was there. He was a thief. As the soldiers were hammering Jesus to the cross, the thief stole the last nail. The one that was supposed to go through Christ's throat. Because of that, Jesus could still talk to His disciples. So Jesus thanked the thief and told him that he and his children and his children's children could steal forever and it would not be a sin. So we're not 'conning' anyone. We're doing the Lord's will."

"I don't remember reading that in the Bible," Crush said.

"We've been written out of history since the very beginning."

Crush didn't know if Lloyd really believed his bullshit or not. "Okay. I can see why you staged that scene in LA. To make Adam feel protective toward her. But why was I there? Why not have Rachel push Udell aside and then take the bullet? Wouldn't that have been better?"

Lloyd shook his head. "I can't hit a moving target. My aim's not that good anymore."

"Besides, we need your help," Rachel said.

"Not interested," Crush said, sliding out of his chair.

"I'll die if you don't," Rachel said.

Crush paused. "You can't con me. I know all your tricks."

"It's not a con. You mentioned the Letters of Transit?"

"You want them back? I still have them."

Lloyd and Rachel exchanged a significant look, and Rachel asked, "Do you remember Mr. Emmerich?"

"I remember his real name wasn't Emmerich," Crush said. "Who was he?"

"Have you ever heard of Meier Lustig?"

Meier Lustig. The same Israeli mob boss who Sterling and Polly said had tried to kill Adam Udell. Crush did his best not to react.

"Yes, I've heard of him."

"When it all went south," Rachel went on, "I tried to hide. Moved to Chicago, to New York. I shook him off."

"But he found me," Lloyd said. "In a trailer park outside of Tucson. His goons broke in while I was sleeping. They tortured me for three days, trying to get me to tell them where she was. It was no use. I would never betray my kin. They were faced with the choice of killing me or letting me go. They let me go, on the condition that I find her and tell her what Lustig wants."

"I don't believe any of this."

"Look at these cigarette burns." Lloyd rolled up his sleeve and showed off some nasty scars.

"I don't doubt somebody tortured you," Crush said. "And I don't doubt they had a very good reason. But I seriously doubt it was Meier Lustig. Why does everybody blame everything on Meier Lustig?"

"Because he wants what Adam Udell has," Lloyd said.

"And what's that?"

"Everything. His whole collection."

"And why is that?"

Lloyd snorted powdered sugar across the table. "Lustig's a nut."

"Lustig's a collector," Rachel corrected him.

"Same difference," Lloyd said. "He wants to have the biggest collection of movie memorabilia in the world."

"And why is that?" Crush repeated.

"Why does anyone want to have anything? So other people can't have it."

"So what exactly does he want from you?" Crush asked Rachel.

"To make up for me trying to sell him fake Letters of Transit, he wants me to get him the rest of Adam's collection," Rachel said.

"Or what?"

"Or he kills me."

"And what exactly is my role in this?"

"Just stay with me. Act like I'm in danger. Protect me. But not too well. Make it so Adam feels like *he* needs to protect me."

"You already got resurrected in your movie. You think if you keep playing the Manic Pixie Dream Girl in Distress he'll leave Polly and marry you? And then you'll get all his stuff?"

"Stranger things have happened," Rachel said.

"And Adam's a nice guy," Lloyd said. "I've spent a few nights drinking with him. He gets up to some pretty wild shit, let me tell you. I'd be proud to call him my son-in-law. So, what do you say, son?"

"I say you want to land Adam Udell, sure. But the part about Meier Lustig threatening you is bullshit."

"It's not," Rachel said. "I give you my word."

"Your word is worth nothing and you know it."

"To a mark, sure. But to you, Crush?"

"How do I know I'm not a mark?"

"I can't believe you'd say that," Rachel said, hurt. Or playing hurt. "What about protecting me?"

"From what? No one's trying to hurt you. No one's trying to hurt Adam. No one's trying to hurt anyone. There's no reason for me to be here."

Rachel slumped in her chair. "I thought we were going to be a team again, Crush."

"Stop by my loft in LA. We can play Pokémon together anytime. Other than that, you're on your own." Crush got up and started to leave. He couldn't help but turn back and say, "Rachel, why don't you stop? You're doing good. Why can't you be happy with what you have? You don't have to keep doing this."

"I'm like a shark, Crush, I gotta keep swimming forward and eating or I'll die."

Crush sighed.

"You know what Robert Browning said," Lloyd chimed

in. " 'A man's reach should exceed his grasp or what's a heaven for?' "

"I don't think Robert Browning was talking about con jobs."

Lloyd gave him a crooked-toothed grin. "We each have to follow our bliss, Caleb."

"I'll see you back at the room, Rachel," Crush said. He walked out onto the bustling sidewalk of Royal Street. It was after eight, and the French Quarter was full of people, tourists mostly, with a smattering of local pickpockets to make it interesting. The Spanish-French architecture, the smells of Creole cooking and beer, the whole sultry atmosphere of the place ought to have intrigued him, but all he wanted to do was get back to his room and figure out how to return to LA as quickly as possible. Preferably without taking an airplane.

Just as he stepped off the curb, it started to rain. Living in LA as he did, it had been a long time since he'd experienced anything like precipitation. Despite the chill in the air, he turned his face up, opened his mouth, and drank it in. To Crush, the mere sight of people opening umbrellas and splashing through puddles was like a vision of an alien world, a strange place where water fell from the sky.

He stood there until he was soaked to the skin, and then he walked back to the hotel, sloshed through the revolving door and went to the elevator, his shoes squeaking and squirting little driblets of water as he tromped across the lobby. Entering Rachel's suite, he stripped off his clothes and took a long, hot shower. He toweled himself off and went into the suite's living room to get some fresh clothes from his bag.

"You do not disappoint, Mr. Rush." Polly was sitting

in the lounge chair by the window, legs crossed, smoking an e-cigarette.

Crush threw his towel over his shoulder. He wasn't in the mood to be modest. "Did I forget to lock the door?"

"I have a passkey," she said. "I'm the power behind the throne, remember?"

He got pants and a shirt out of his bag. "How would the king feel about you being in here?"

She shrugged. "He plays. I play. We have an understanding."

"You two have been together for a long time. Why haven't you gotten married?"

"Adam doesn't believe in marriage."

"And you?"

"I believe in Adam."

He put on his pants. "Good for you."

"Don't get dressed on my account."

He pulled on a dark blue T-shirt. "I have a rule. I don't get naked with people who are paying me."

She pouted a little. "You won't make an exception?"

"If I made an exception for you, I'd have to make it for everyone. It would be exhausting. Besides, I hardly know you."

"Don't you find that's the best time to get naked with someone? When you hardly know them? They hold so much promise."

"And after you get to know them?"

"They're usually a disappointment." She got up and went to the door. "What if I fired you? Would you have time for me then?"

"Then I'd have to look for work."

She pouted. "You're no fun."

"I used to be fun. Now I'm professional."

"You don't know what you're missing," she said with a smile as she walked out the door.

Crush had a pretty good idea of what he was missing. He went and took another shower. A cold one this time. He pulled out the sofa bed in the suite and got under the sheets. Then he got out of bed and put on some boxers, just in case someone surprised him. It was shaping up to be that kind of night. Rachel was still out, but rather than wait up for her, he switched off the lights and meditated. Despite the thoughts he had whirling through his head, he was asleep in a matter of minutes. Meditation was a great gift, Crush reflected, as he drifted off to sleep.

Even when Rachel came in and switched on the light, he just pulled the foam pillow over his head and went right on sleeping. He didn't really wake up until almost one-thirty. That's when he heard a loud thump, a shattering crash, and a groan from the room next door.

He sat up and listened. There was no follow-up. No sound of someone scuffling. No one getting up and stumbling around to shake it off. Just dead silence. He got out of bed and knocked on the wall.

"Hey," Crush shouted, "are you okay?" He went over his mental map of their rooms in the hotel. Byron Douglas, movie star, occupied that room. "Byron?" He pressed his ear to the wall and listened. Nothing. He dashed over to his satchel, pulled on a T-shirt, and rooted around until he found Zerbe's dry-erase marker. Time to see if it really worked.

He went out into the hall. The door to the Wolfe Suite opened a crack. Crush ignored it and hammered on the door of Byron's suite. "Byron? Are you there?"

Another door opened and Polly came out, bleary-eyed, wrapping a robe around herself. "What are you doing?"

"Does Byron have seizures?"

"No, I don't think so. What's wrong?"

"Somebody collapsed in there. They're not answering." He knelt down by the doorknob, took the cap off the dry-erase marker, and inserted it into the DC power port located on the underside of the keycard lock. He waited a second and tried the door handle. It opened easily.

"Where'd you get that?" Polly asked.

"A friend made it for me," he said as he stepped into the Hemingway Suite. Byron lay in a heap by the sofa, a lamp with a shattered bulb resting by his side. Crush hurried to him, reached under him, and felt his chest. He was still breathing, but just barely. With Polly's help he flipped him over. Byron was nude. And a hypodermic needle was sticking out of his stomach.

CHAPTER NINE

Polly reached down and plucked the needle out of Byron's stomach while Crush started performing mouth-to-mouth on him. Between breaths, he snapped to Polly, "Call 911."

She picked up the hotel phone and dialed. "Has a Dr. ten Berge checked in?"

"What are you doing?" Crush asked. Byron's pupils were dilated; his breathing was imperceptible.

"Could you connect me with her room?" Polly went on.

"Call 911!" he repeated.

"Alva? We have a little problem in Room 715. The Hemingway Suite." Polly turned to Crush. "How is he?"

"He's not breathing," Crush said.

"Byron has stopped breathing." Polly sounded calm, as if she was explaining that Byron had a slightly annoying toothache. "Do hurry." She hung up. "Alva is quicker than the paramedics."

"And safer?"

"There's no reason to involve the authorities, if we can help it."

Seconds later, Dr. ten Berge came through the door, wearing a green kimono over gray pajamas and carrying the proverbial black bag of old-movie doctors. As she knelt by Byron's side, she had the same severe expression as she'd had at the poolside examining Rachel's wound. Crush wondered if she ever relaxed. She checked Byron's eyes and listened to his breathing. Or lack of breathing. "What was he taking?" she asked.

"HGH" Polly said.

"Is that all?"

"All I know of."

HGH. Human growth hormone. Crush knew about it. It was the new steroids. Bodybuilders at his gym took it, and it was all the rage among aging action stars. Two shots of HGH a day and, with diet and exercise, you could become the ripped, shredded, well-defined physical specimen all men needed to be in the movies of the early twenty-first century. Nobody took off his shirt and looked like Dean Martin these days.

The side effects? Only joint pain and an increased risk of diabetes. Oh, and also cancer. Colon cancer. Prostate cancer. Hodgkin's lymphoma. You name it. But that was rare. That was in the distant future. The movie role, that was here and now.

"HGH doesn't do this," Dr. ten Berge said, pulling a mask with an inflatable bag out of her satchel. "We have to bag him." She sat on the floor, hovering over him. "Lift his head and put it on my lap."

Crush adjusted Byron's head while she put the mask on his face and pumped the bag against her leg. It forced air into Byron's lungs, and his chest rose and fell. She did it again and turned to Crush. "Hello again," she said without a hint of a smile. "Tell me, do you know how to perform chest compressions?"

Crush nodded.

"Time it with my pumping of the bag," she said.

He pressed on Byron's chest the way he'd learned to do in the Marines, where he'd done it more times than he cared to remember, in places he would just as soon forget.

They worked on Byron for what felt like hours but was twenty minutes by Crush's watch. Byron was breathing now, but it was purely mechanical; when they stopped pumping, he didn't breathe at all. They kept pumping. Dr. ten Berge was focused and determined, and Crush worked with her as if they'd done this a thousand times before.

Polly paced about the room for a while and then disappeared into the bathroom. Ten Berge gestured for Crush to stop pumping. He looked at Byron's chest. It was rising and falling on its own.

"You can rest," she said. "I'll keep bagging him."

She kept pumping the bag and Crush lay back on the floor, surprisingly exhausted from the effort of keeping this man alive. Polly came out of the bathroom. "I found this in the trash can." She was holding a small injection vial in her hand. "It doesn't have a label, but it's full."

"Look around for another one," ten Berge said, still pumping the bag. "It would help to know what he took."

Crush went into the bathroom and checked Byron's Dopp kit. No sign of another bottle. Looking in the mirror, he noticed some smudges, as if someone had run a finger over it. He breathed on the mirror and something that looked like the capital letters FC appeared.

When he went back to the bedroom, Polly was rooting around behind a chair and stood up, holding another little bottle, this one empty. "Is this it?" she asked.

"What does it say on the label?" ten Berge asked.

"Sermorelin GHRP-Six."

The doctor shook her head. "That's HGH. That didn't do this."

Crush took the vial from Polly and examined it. Byron moaned and his eyes opened. Dr. ten Berge lifted the mask from his face. "How are you feeling?" she asked.

"What happened?" Byron asked, groggy.

"What did you take?"

"Just some H. I forgot my dose so I got out of bed and took a shot. That's the last thing I remember."

"You had a bad reaction," Polly said.

"You stopped breathing," Dr. ten Berge said.

"You mean I died?" Byron said, his voice trembling.

"Not quite," the doctor said.

"But almost? I was almost dead?"

Dr. ten Berge shrugged. "If you want."

"Wow," Byron said. "I had a near-death experience!" There was more than a little bit of pride in his voice.

Crush looked closely at the label on the vial. It was coming loose at one corner. Carefully, he peeled it off, revealing another label underneath it. He showed it to Dr. ten Berge as she packed up her ambu bag. "Propofol," she read from the bottle.

"Shit," Byron said. "Isn't that the stuff that killed Michael Jackson?"

"Yes. It's an anesthetic," Dr. ten Berge said. "Very powerful. Very dangerous. A small dose can cause unconsciousness and loss of memory. A bit more and you stop breathing and die."

"I died for a while," Byron said, improving the story as he went along. "Wow!"

"Adam calls it his 'milk of amnesia,'" Polly said.

"Is Adam still taking it?" ten Berge asked, her tone, if possible, sounding even harsher than usual.

"It's the only way he can sleep when he's in production. You know that," Polly said. "We're very careful with it."

"You better be," ten Berge said. "Now go. I have to do some maintenance on Mr. Douglas."

"What maintenance?" Byron asked, a little worried.

"Let it be a surprise," the doctor said.

Polly headed for the door. Crush held back. "Byron, do the letters FC mean anything to you?"

"Not really. Father Christmas? Fielder's choice? Why?"

"It was written on your mirror."

Byron shrugged. "Maybe the maid is a soccer fan. You sure it didn't say FC Barcelona? You know, football club?"

"Maybe." Crush and Polly walked out into the hall.

"Nothing seems emptier than a hotel hallway at two in the morning," Polly said. "I don't know about you, but I could use a drink."

"Okay."

"Don't tell me you want an iced tea."

What Crush wanted was a shot of bourbon, but as they sat down in the Tennessee Williams Suite and Polly poured herself some tequila, he made himself settle for a three-dollar bottle of water.

Polly reclined on the sofa, languidly, and looked over at Crush in his boxers. "It seems like I've seldom seen you fully dressed, Mr. Rush. Why is that?"

"Just your bad luck. Ordinarily, I wear a top hat and tails."

"Classy. So what was that trick with the dry-erase marker and the lock?"

"Oh, that. My stepbrother has a lot of time on his hands. He made that with something called a microcontroller and a resistor or something. I didn't pay much attention."

"But it worked."

"Yes," Crush said. "Although *you* wouldn't have needed it. You have a passkey, remember?"

"I didn't think of that."

"How many bottles of that stuff do you have?"

"What stuff?"

"Propofol."

"We're on location for two weeks, so fourteen."

"And if I were to count the bottles, how many would I find?"

"Fourteen," Polly said. "Or are you suggesting one is missing?"

"If Byron didn't bring the Propofol, it had to come from somewhere."

"And you think it came from our stash? I assure you, I take excellent care of it."

"Could you check?"

She flounced off the sofa and into the bathroom. She came out with a Dopp kit filled with vials of the precious milk of amnesia. "Thirteen bottles—one *is* missing."

"How 'bout that?" Crush said.

"Do you think *I* did it? Why would I try to kill the star of my new movie?"

"*Your* new movie? Don't you mean your boyfriend's new movie?"

"Our new movie then. Why would I want to damage that?"

"I don't know. Maybe you have something against Byron. Or maybe you want to get back at Adam. Ruin his movie. He isn't exactly a model boyfriend."

"Oh, please," she said. "The jealous woman wronged? I don't *do* jealousy."

"Rachel seems to get under your skin."

"I don't trust her. Should I? Don't you think she's up to something?"

"She hasn't slept with Adam, you know."

"That's what I mean. If he just dipped his wick, he'd be over her and move on to the next one. That's his way. But she's too smart for that. She keeps him wanting more."

"But you're not jealous?"

She smiled a lovely smile. "Not jealous. Concerned. She's a formidable rival."

"Like in *Game of Thrones*?"

Polly laughed. "More like *Deadwood*. But Rachel wasn't the one who was poisoned, was she?"

"No, she wasn't."

"So why would I try to kill Byron?"

"I didn't say you did. It's just that you had access to the drug. You had access to Byron's room. And I notice you're not calling the police and reporting this incident."

"It hadn't even occurred to me. That's strange, isn't it?"

"It *is* strange."

"I guess we live in such a rarified atmosphere that we play by our own rules. We don't think about things like the police."

"Who's 'we'?"

"Adam. Me. All of us. Do you think I should call?"

"It's not for me to say."

"I think I should call." She moved to the hotel phone and lifted the receiver. Then she paused. "Although..."

He'd been waiting for that. "Yes?"

"Well, it will cause so much disturbance. It will change the story."

"The story?"

"Adam is making the sequel to one of the most successful films ever made. The internet is buzzing with rumors about the new script. About whether or not the

Enforcer really learned to love. About whether or not the rebellion really defeated the Dictator. About whether or not the Enforcer and Marnie get together."

"Marnie?"

"That's Rachel's character. Didn't you see it?"

"I don't go to the movies much."

She looked more offended by that than when Crush had all but accused her of trying to kill Byron. "Well, it left a lot of unanswered questions."

"Why? Didn't you have the answers?"

"Leaving unanswered questions is the thing these days. It keeps people coming back for more."

"I find that frustrating. I like stories that end."

"Welcome to the twenty-first century. Stories never end now. They just lead to sequels until they stop making money. Anyway, *that's* what people are talking about. That's what we *want* them to talk about. Not about this. Not about who tried to kill Byron. If anybody did try to kill him."

"Didn't they?"

"Well, they wanted to send a message, of course. Message received. But no harm was really done, right?"

"Because we broke in and saved him."

"But somebody would have, right? It was just Meier's way of trying to scare us."

"Meier again."

"Well, who else could it have been?"

"That's the question, isn't it?" Crush got up and went to the door "Tell me, did Adam have access to the Propofol?"

"Well, sure. Our suites are adjoining. He comes and goes. But why would Adam want to hurt his star?"

"He probably wouldn't. But it seems to me that the only people who could have done it are you and him."

"And you. You could have gotten into this room with your magic lock picker, taken the Propofol, gotten into Byron's room the same way, and substituted the drugs."

"That's true. Only I didn't know you had the Propofol and I didn't know Byron took HGH."

"Maybe not. But Rachel knew. And aren't you working for Rachel?"

"I don't really know who I'm working for anymore," he said as he opened the door and walked out of the room.

CHAPTER TEN

reakfast is served," Rachel said, after the room service delivery had come and gone. "How was your night?"

"I've had better." Crush sat up in the pullout bed and ran his tongue over his scummy teeth.

"I noticed you went visiting last night," she said, pouring a cup of coffee. "Have any fun?"

"Not particularly," he said, getting up to go brush his teeth.

"When are you heading back to Los Angeles, Crush?" She still pronounced the city the old fashioned way, with a hard "g." Some things never changed.

"I don't know if I am," he said. She'd ordered him a bowl of oatmeal. That was another thing that hadn't changed.

"You going to stick around?"

"I think so."

"Groovy."

There was a knock on the door and Rachel went to answer it. Byron stood in the doorway, smiling brightly. "Did Rush tell you? I died last night!"

"You died?"

"Well, almost. I had a near-death experience! It was awe inspiring."

"I was getting ready to tell her," Crush said. Then he ran through the events of last night, quickly and without embellishment.

"But that's just the facts," Byron said, pulling up a chair. "That doesn't tell you what really happened! I died! I stopped breathing!"

"He *did* stop breathing," Crush confirmed.

"See? And I had an out-of-body experience! Felt myself floating over my body. I could see Crush and Dr. ten Berge working on me!"

"You didn't mention that last night," Crush said.

"Well, I was in shock! But I saw it! I was floating over the room."

"Toward a bright light?" Rachel asked.

"You laugh, but yes! I looked up and I saw this bright light, and it was calling to me. Not with words, but with *feelings*! It was a beautiful feeling! Like it was calling me home! Then, all of a sudden, I zoomed back into my body and I was looking up at Dr. ten Berge!"

"Must have been a disappointment," Rachel said. "After that cosmic light calling you and all, to end up staring at Alva."

"You're making fun of me, but it was a life-changing experience. I'm a new man. I've been born again."

"You found God?" Crush asked.

"I'm not sure about that. I'll have to take some time to sift through it all. Figure out what it means. Is anybody drinking this tomato juice?"

"It's mine, but you can have it," Rachel said.

Byron picked it up and drank it down in one gulp. "There! I never liked tomato juice before. I loved that! It's a new beginning for me, I tell you!" He got up and walked out of the room, leaving the door ajar. Actor that he was, he knew a good exit line. Rachel walked over and closed the door.

"Is *that* why you're staying?" Rachel asked Crush.

"You didn't switch those drugs did you?" Crush asked Rachel.

"Of course not. Why would I want to kill Byron? I like Byron."

"You do?"

"Yeah, he cracks me up."

"Maybe you knew I'd save him. Maybe that's why you wanted me here?"

She thought about that. "It's kind of a stretch. How would I know he'd fall down and knock over that lamp? It doesn't track, Crush. And why would I want to poison him anyway?"

"To keep Adam off balance?"

She thought about that one, too. "I like that. That would work. But it's too risky. I mean, what if Byron died? Then I'd be out of a job."

"There'll be other jobs."

"But not with Adam. The whole point of this is Adam."

Now it was Crush's turn to think. "Are you in love with Adam Udell?"

"What kind of question is that to ask a grifter? You know we never let our hearts get involved in the game."

"But what if you did, this one time. That's what happens in the movies. The stone-cold grifter falls for her mark. If it's a comedy, they live happily ever after. If it's a crime story, she ends up dead."

"This isn't a movie, Crush."

"You once told me it was all a movie. I didn't believe you then. Now I'm not so sure."

"So why are you sticking around? To protect me? Or to protect Adam from me?"

"Let's just say that I'd like to protect everyone from

everyone."

"So you're like Superman? Or Zorro? Hey, you'd make a good Zorro."

There was a series of rapid knocks on the door and Rachel swung it open to reveal Adam Udell standing there with a smile. "Read-through in twenty minutes," he said. "And don't mumble your way through it. I want you to deliver."

"Adam," Rachel said, "that speech worked last time, when I was just a nobody. But now I'm a star. I'll mumble if I want to."

"Do you want to?"

"No, I want to deliver."

"Atta girl." He started to leave and then paused. "You gonna join us, Crush?"

"I wasn't planning on it."

"Plan on it. You're the closest thing to the Enforcer I've ever seen in real life. Hey, you can be a consultant. I'll put you on the payroll."

"That's not necessary," Crush said.

"Consider it done. Be there." And he was gone.

Crush and Rachel were silent for a moment. Then Rachel asked, "How many people are paying you now, Crush?"

"You. Polly. And now, I guess, Paramount Pictures."

Rachel shook her head and laughed. "And you say you're not a con man."

◎

The William Faulkner Suite was set up as an impromptu salon, the sofas arranged in a circle, with an easy chair at the apex of the makeshift amphitheater. In this throne,

Adam Udell held court, cajoling and chatting with Rachel
and the rest of the cast—the rest of the cast except for Byron Douglas, who was late. Twenty minutes later, when
he still hadn't shown up, Rachel got up and walked out
of the suite.

Crush spotted Sterling, as rangy and dashing as ever,
getting himself some coffee at the refreshment table. He
looked like an aging toreador coming around for one last
look at the bulls. "What's happening?" Crush asked him.

"It's standard operating procedure. The usual pissing
contest. Two stars seeing who can be the last to show up
for the reading. Adam will teach them who's boss."

After about forty-five minutes, the small talk had died
out and the dozen or so people, some of whom Crush
recognized as character actors from TV and movies but
whose names he didn't know, sat around with scripts
held limply in their hands, waiting.

Fifty-five minutes late, Byron came bursting through
the door, smiling brightly. "Good morning everybody.
Let's get started!"

Adam raised his right hand above his head, palm out.
"Not yet," he said in a low, ominous tone.

"We're waiting for Rachel," Polly explained.

"Oh," Byron said, shaking his head, "our little discov-
ery has turned into a prima donna. Let me know when
she deigns to show up." And he turned on his heel to
walk out.

"Stay right there, Chester," Adam said, calling Byron
by the name of his character in his former sitcom, *Family
Practice*, as if to remind him of his humble station in life.
"You're not going anywhere."

"Why not?" Byron asked, treating it like a joke.

"Because if you walk out that door, I'll fire you and

replace you in a heartbeat."

"Really? With who?"

"I have Chris Pratt and Chris Evans on the hook. They're both younger and prettier than you are."

Byron laughed, but he didn't walk out. "Anybody else named Chris? Hemsworth maybe? Or Pine? How about Walken—he's due for a comeback."

Just then, Rachel walked in. "She makes her entrance!" Byron said. "Are you going to replace *her*, Adam?"

Rachel didn't skip a beat. "I got tired of waiting for you, Chester. I went to take a crap."

"Stop it!" Adam shouted at Rachel. "You're nothing more than a club digger I picked up on a whim." He turned on Byron. "And you, you're just a washed-up TV hack on steroids. Neither of you is indispensable! *I'm* not indispensable! What's indispensable is the movie! What's indispensable is the fucking *Rage Machine*! Do you *understand?!*"

Crush would have thought Adam's conniption fit was funny if he hadn't seen the reaction it got from the room. Everyone was trembling and staring, as if God, or at least Donald Trump, was unleashing his holy fury in front of them. *"Do you understand!!!???"* the director screamed, spit flying from his lips.

"I understand," Rachel said, lowering her eyes. It may have been part of her act, but it was still arresting for Crush to see her so cowed.

Byron, on the other hand, was still trying to save face by treating it as a joke. "I hear you, Chief—you don't have to get your thong in a knot."

Adam leapt from his easy-chair throne, throwing the script to the floor. He began to yell right in Byron's face. "You think I'm *joking*?! You think this is *funny*?! This is a hundred-million-dollar picture and you just wasted an hour of my time, you laugh-track whore! Do you want me to show everybody how tough you really are? I'll do it! I'll throw down with you, right this second! *Are you man enough!?*"

Byron stared at the much smaller man who was poised before him, ready to strike. And he backed down. "All right, Chief, it won't happen again," he muttered.

"Damn right, it won't! Because I will walk off this movie myself if I don't see everyone, and I mean everyone, giving it their fucking all! And I mean every bit of themselves! I expect people to *die* for this movie!"

There was utter silence in the room.

"But, of course, not until we've shot your last scene." This was followed by one nervous laugh from the back of the room. Adam jabbed a finger in the direction of the laughter. "That *was* a joke! I don't care *when* you die, as long as you live and breathe this motion picture! We're all in this together! Now. Page one. Fade in."

Crush glanced at Sterling next to him, who nodded, smiling, as if to say "That's how it's done." Scare the hell out of everyone. Make everyone think you're crazy. Take charge.

They read the script aloud. It had something to do with a dystopian future (what other kind was there these days?) and a civil war between the haves and the have-nots. There were a lot of gunfights and knife fights and very few scenes with actual dialogue. Without having seen the first movie, Crush was at a loss to know the good guys from the bad guys and found his mind wandering to other, better movie plots to pass the two hours until the script ended with the requisite cliffhanger ending.

The applause from the cast as the scripts were flipped

closed seemed heartfelt, so Crush joined in. "There," Adam said. "Now let's go out and make this. I'd give a pep talk but you don't need it. You're all the best or I wouldn't have hired you. Don't prove me wrong."

He stood up and walked into the bedroom, gesturing with his script. "Crush, Sterling, Rachel, Byron. In here."

Crush was a bit startled to be included in this meeting, whatever it was, and more startled by being given first billing. Sterling patted him on the back and whispered, "You're in the inner circle now. Watch your back."

They went into the bedroom, where they found Adam already stretched out on the bed, peeling his shirt off and throwing it in the corner. "I sweat through five of these a day," he explained to Crush, as if Crush cared.

Rachel and Byron were the last ones in. Polly shut the door behind them.

"All right," Adam said, "we break the cherry on this puppy tonight. First scene is midnight in the graveyard, where Marnie and the Enforcer have a meeting with the Senator and discover that he's in bed with the Dictator."

"Right," Rachel said. "In the rain?"

"It's always in the rain. You have any thoughts, Crush?"

Crush was brought up short. "About what?"

"The Enforcer's supposed to be protecting Marnie. What would you do?"

"Well, I wouldn't have her meet anybody in a graveyard at midnight in the rain. That's just stupid."

"The Dictator has surveillance everywhere else."

"So his twenty-third-century surveillance can't see in the dark in the rain?"

"No. And graveyards are off the grid, too."

"How come?"

Adam was getting rankled. "They just are."

"Can I put in a word here?" Byron said. Crush had been surprised and impressed by Byron's performance during the reading. Dropping his voice a few octaves and evoking a husky whisper that reminded Crush of Eastwood or Bronson at their best, he really made a convincing Enforcer. Whatever an Enforcer was.

"Sure," said Adam, not sounding like he meant a word he was saying, "that's what we're here for. Let's hear it."

"I'm not sure about the amount of violence in this script," Byron said.

"I think there's enough," Adam said. "We'll get a hard R."

"No, that's not it," Byron went on. "I think there's too much. I mean, look at the world today. What are we really saying to people?"

"I don't follow."

"Well I mean, look at the news these days. There's all these mass shootings and things. In real life, I mean. And what are we saying with this movie? That guns and shooting are the solutions to our problems? That they save the day? Is that really a responsible thing to be telling people?"

Adam just stared at him. "Who have you been talking to? Have you been talking to your ex-wife? You know she's crazy."

"No," Byron said. "I've been talking to God."

Everyone stared at Byron now.

"And when was this, Byron?" Adam asked.

"Last night. You heard about that, right? You heard about how I died?"

"I heard you had a stupid accident with your meds."

"It was no accident. It was fate."

"You didn't mention talking to God when you told us about it this morning," Rachel said.

"I only remembered it when I was in the shower afterward."

"If I talked to Our Lord and Savior I don't think it would slip my mind," Adam said.

"It's a hard thing to comprehend. It takes time," Byron said. He wasn't talking in exclamation points anymore.

"What form did God take exactly?" Polly asked. "Yahweh? Jesus? Mohammed? Cthulhu?"

"Peace," Byron said. "It was a sense of unutterable peace."

"Unutterable?" Adam repeated. "You seem to be uttering it now."

"I don't want to kill all these people in this movie," Byron said. "It just doesn't seem right. Can't we think of another way to do it?"

"Another way to overthrow a totalitarian regime?" Adam asked.

"Gandhi did it."

"People don't want to pay fifteen dollars a ticket to see you in a diaper, starving yourself in IMAX 3D," Adam said.

"Just think about it," Byron said.

"Byron, this is a comic-book picture." Adam spoke calmly. "In comic books things go 'boom,' 'pow,' 'splat.' Bad guys die in horrible, spectacular ways and the audience cheers. And it's okay, because everybody knows it's pretend. It's catharsis. Look it up. Now, you want to go make a biopic about Martin Luther King next, have at it. You can play James Earl Ray and shoot him with a squirt gun. Is that nonviolent enough for you?"

"You're not even considering..."

"I'm not. This discussion is closed. Unless you want

me to get Chris Pratt on the phone. The Enforcer can always regenerate as a younger man, remember?"

"People expect to see me as the Enforcer." Byron was holding his own, but just barely.

"And people expect the Enforcer to kill people. He was genetically designed to kill people. Remember?"

"But wouldn't it be great if we said he could defeat that genetic programming? If we said he had free will?"

Adam leapt from the bed. "I'll think about it. Now I'm bored. I'll see you at the cemetery at five tonight. Be prepared to kill people." And he walked into the bathroom.

Byron was left standing there, with his mouth hanging open. He turned to Crush. "You get what I'm saying, don't you?"

"I get it," Crush said.

Sterling spoke up. "Let him think about it for a piece. You know his process."

"Yeah," Byron said. "He'll think about it and then decide to ignore me. Well, I won't be ignored." He turned and walked out of the room.

"I didn't see that coming," said Rachel.

"When production starts on a movie," Polly said, "the shit always hits the fan. You just never know what shit or what fan."

CHAPTER ELEVEN

In a Motel 6 way out on Gentilly Road, Rachel's father, Lloyd Fury, was just waking up. He wasn't sleeping in the bed; that was what they expected. Besides, he knew what went on in Motel 6 beds. Nasty stuff. No, the floor suited him just fine. It was firm and he couldn't roll off it. And if anybody came looking for him, he could quickly roll into the bathroom and out the window. Lloyd Fury always needed an exit strategy.

Lloyd had looked over his shoulder ever since he was a kid, pulling Three Card Monte and Follow the Lady on the streets of Houston. He'd worked his way up through Pig in the Poke and Thai Gem scams to being one of the best psychic surgeons in the Southwest. Once he lost his eye (sometimes his victims caught up with him), he turned lemons into lemonade by being one of the best "glim droppers" in North America. Maybe he'd try pulling that one this week, if he could get Rachel to play along.

He'd go into a diner (Frank's Eats down the street looked promising) and claim he'd lost his "glim" (his glass eye) there. Lots of pointing to his vacant socket and even opening it, to the disgust of the man or woman behind the counter. Then he'd offer a big reward to anyone who found it. Five hundred dollars, maybe a thousand. Lloyd would sense what would be enough but not too much for these suckers to believe. Then he'd leave, but not before giving his cell phone number to the guy behind the counter.

After a little while, Rachel comes in, orders lunch, and "finds" the glass eye on the floor under her table. The guy behind the counter offers to take it and return it to the poor man who lost it. And keep the reward for himself. Rachel then says she wants to return it, if he'll just give her the contact number. The guy behind the counter sees the reward going out the window, so he offers fifty dollars for the eye. Rachel refuses until she gets the guy up to, say, two hundred or three hundred dollars, depending on the atmosphere and how desperate the guy is.

Then she leaves with the money and the guy calls the number, which turns out to be a phone-sex company specializing in gay BDSM. True, Lloyd is out one perfectly good glass eye, but that's not so bad. He has a boxful of them in his suitcase. And three hundred dollars in his pocket.

But he knew he shouldn't be daydreaming about other cons. He should be focusing on the one at hand. The long con. The one that he could retire on. Not that Lloyd ever thought he'd retire. He loved the game too much to ever give it up entirely. But he wouldn't be working from need. To be honest, that worried him a bit. Would he be as good—would he be the old Lloyd Fury—it he weren't just a little bit desperate?

There was a knock on the door. Lloyd reacted before he thought, rolling over to the bathroom door to make his quick escape. *Who am I running from?* he wondered, as he climbed up to and out the bathroom window. The list of possibilities was longer than he cared to admit. But he knew this—nobody who knocked on motel-room doors brought good news.

The ground was still wet from the rainy night before. He crept around the back of the motel. He'd been sleeping in his clothes, with his keys and wallet (containing a fake ID under the name of George Kaplan) in his pocket— he always slept that way, the better to make a clean getaway—so all he had to do was make it to his rental car and drive off. *But what if it was Rachel?* he thought. She might have a change of plan she wanted to run by him.

But wouldn't she have texted him first? He pulled out his burner phone. No texts. But what if her cell phone had been compromised? Best to peek around the corner of the building, just to check. Besides, if it was someone else at the door, wouldn't it behoove him to know who that someone else was?

So he poked his head around the ice machine to catch a glimpse of whomever was at the door of his room. Only his forehead and his eyes cleared the corner. That was all the shooter needed. A single shot clipped the top of Lloyd's head, sending a spray of blood and brains across the parking lot. As he fell to the pavement, dead, his glass eye rolled under the ice chest. A glim dropper to the last.

CHAPTER TWELVE

New Orleans police officers were bagging George Kaplan's body and having trouble notifying his next of kin in Sacramento. The home address on his driver's license turned out to be a Jack in the Box off Route 80. Inside his motel room, they located his suitcase, which had two hidden pockets. One contained fifteen glass eyes. The other held twelve driver's licenses, each with a different name and address.

None of them were for Lloyd Fury.

While this was going on, Adam stepped outside the Louisiane Hotel and took a deep breath of New Orleans stink. "God, I love this town." Crush followed, stepping over a puddle and walking across the crowded street. It was warmer today, in the seventies and, though clouds filled the sky, it didn't feel like it was going to rain.

A few minutes before, Adam had rapped on Rachel's door, wearing his usual uniform of black jacket and black T-shirt over black jeans, and asked Crush if he wanted to walk over to the location and check it out. Rachel was buried deep in her script pages for tonight's scene and waved him on. Crush had no choice but to go.

"I used to live here," Adam said as he dodged traffic and got to the other side of Royal Street. "In my boho days."

Crush got the feeling he was expected to respond.

"Did you?"

"Everybody knows that. Didn't you Google me?"

"I don't Google people."

"You should take it up. Anyway, I used to play in a band at a Bourbon Street strip club. The Convulsions, we were called. Straight-up punk. And I did those Ghost Walking Tours on my off nights. When I led the tourists past the Ursuline Convent, I had strippers in bloody nuns' habits come wailing out of nowhere. Used to scare the shit out of them. Literally. Sometimes they'd shit themselves they were so scared."

"Did they like that?"

"They got their money's worth. That's all I want to do with my movies. To make people shit themselves in their seats."

"Literally?"

"Sure. Why would I want to wuss out? I want them to have to fumigate the theaters after they show my pictures."

"Well, you have your Oscar acceptance speech all ready for this weekend then."

"I know I'm not going to win that." They turned a corner and walked past a voodoo shop. "I don't even know if I'm going to go. It's the weekend. I'm in the middle of production. Besides, it's just a beauty contest. Fuck it."

"I don't know you very well, Adam, but one thing I do know. You're going to go to the Oscars."

"Yeah, I suppose you're right," he said, with a faraway look in his eyes. "They'll give it to Ridley Scott for his Holocaust movie. Holocaust movies always win. I should make a fucking Holocaust movie next. That would really make them shit themselves."

Adam walked in silence for a while. Crush was grateful for that. It didn't last long enough. Adam stopped and turned to Crush abruptly. "If you're supposed to be protecting Rachel, what are you doing with me?"

"You invited me."

"But you didn't have to come. You don't mind pissing me off. We've established that. Do you know why you're with me?"

"Tell me."

"You're with me because Polly is paying you to keep an eye on me, right?"

"Why would she do that?"

"Because she doesn't trust me. She thinks I'm falling for Rachel."

"Does she?"

"What are you, a shrink? You keep answering my questions with questions."

"Do I?"

"Fuck it. I'm tired of walking." Adam pulled out his iPhone and called for a car to drive them to Lafayette Cemetery Number Four on the outskirts of the Vieux Carré. "I could have you barred from the set, you know," he said as he slid the phone back into his pocket. "I could bar you from New Orleans. Are you going to answer me? Is my girlfriend paying you?"

"Yes. But not to watch you. To protect you."

"From what?"

"She thinks someone is trying to kill you."

The Town Car pulled up and they climbed in the back. Adam didn't even speak to the driver. He didn't have to.

"Do you know what movie I'm doing next?" Adam said, changing the subject.

"I don't care," Crush said.

"*Don Quixote.* Do you know it?"

"I've never read it. I know it's about a crazy knight. And windmills."

"Right. But this is a science fiction version of *Don Quixote*. The windmills are going to be space stations."

"Is that better?"

"Of course it's better. It's in space." He was quiet for a moment. Then he spoke. "I don't need protection."

"So no one wants to kill you?"

"Let them try," he said, pulling open his jacket to reveal a leather shoulder holster. He drew a pistol out and held it up. "It's a Beretta 92FS. The same kind Chow Yun-Fat used in *The Killer*."

Crush looked at it. "I don't like guns. They have this nasty tendency to go off and shoot people."

"You don't carry a gun?"

"No, I don't."

"Then I could kill you right now," Adam said, pointing the Beretta at Crush. "Even though you're bigger than me."

Crush looked at him steadily. "Go ahead and try."

They locked eyes for moment. "Naw, I was just joking." Adam laughed and put the gun back under his jacket. "I could have if I'd wanted to, though."

"Keep telling yourself that."

The car stopped, and they got out at Cemetery Number Four. Like the more famous Cemetery Number One, Number Four was enclosed by an ominously stained and weathered wall of whitewashed brick. A fleet of trucks and RVs was parked all around the open wrought iron gate that separated them from this city of the dead. They walked through it, elbowed by crowds of grips and Teamsters who were transforming this already spooky setting into something more cinematically ominous.

Inside it really was like a city: narrow, winding streets with all manner of crypts, like little cottages, lining the way. New Orleans was built on a swamp, and swamps tend to disgorge things that are buried in the usual way. So here the dead are lodged in above-ground sepulchers for two years before their bones are scooped to the side to make room for more. *Very efficient*, Crush thought.

Adam went off to talk intently with his director of photography and came back smiling. "I was right. No rain tonight, thank God."

"I thought you wanted it to rain," Crush said.

Adam shook his head. "Real rain doesn't show up on the screen. You need movie rain." He pointed to a rigging of pipes that was being set up above them. "It's all make-believe. Come on. I want to show you something."

He took off through the narrow streets of tombs and mausoleums without looking back to see if Crush was following. Adam ran the maze of the necropolis and Crush moved to keep up. They'd left the hustle and bustle of the movie location behind them. The sun was setting. They were alone in a graveyard, coming on nightfall. Crush wasn't superstitious, but he felt the hair on the back of his neck stand up.

"I'm going to move to New Orleans when I retire," Adam said. "Make personal movies on my iPhone. Fuck the studios and the industry in general."

"This industry has been pretty good to you, hasn't it?" Crush said.

"You have no idea how much it chews you up and spits you out. I fucking hate it. You know, the funny thing is, he's right."

"Who's right?"

"Byron. There *is* too much violence in this damn

movie. It's totally irresponsible. We're contributing to the decline of civilization." He turned to Crush, full of energy now. "And how 'bout that for an ending? The Enforcer puts down his gun and says 'No more killing, and it starts with me.' Then, of course, he gets mowed down by the Dictator's guns. But he sets an example. And it spreads. And, in time, peace and justice prevail. That would be a beautiful ending...and a total box office bomb. People don't want difficult ideas. They want simple, visceral pabulum. And we give it to them."

"Why?" Crush asked.

"Because we're whores. Highly paid, highly skilled whores. We give the client the wet dream he desires. And you know why?"

Crush didn't have to answer. Adam was on a roll and he didn't really care if anyone was listening.

"Because we love it. We love to give them exactly what they want. It makes us feel powerful. We're stuck in a sick S&M relationship with the audience. It's like *Fifty Shades of* fucking *Grey* times ten."

They'd walked a long way and left the film crew far, far behind when Adam stopped at a turn in the narrow road. "All right. Enough of that. This is what I wanted to show you. Prepare to be impressed." He led Crush around the corner with his outstretched hand, like the Crypt Keeper in the old comic books.

Crush walked around the lichen-covered, battered wall of the nearest tomb and into a cleared area. There, in the middle of a little square, sat a gleaming white pyramid of polished marble. Unlike the crumbling crypts that surrounded it, the pyramid looked brand new, as if it had been recently stuck there, like a shiny new Lego piece among a pile of decaying Lincoln Logs.

The pyramid towered over Crush. One of its plain white walls gleamed so brightly from the reflected sunset that he had to squint to look at it. "It's amazing, isn't it?" Adam was looking at it with undisguised wonder. There was a brass door in the center of the north wall, engraved with a name Crush couldn't make out.

"Some eccentric rich guy decided he wanted to be buried here," Adam said. "So he built this. Can you imagine how much this cost? And the incredible thing is, he's not even dead yet. He's not even old. He just built this thing to wait for him. Isn't that eerie?"

"Who built it?" Crush asked.

"Me!" Adam said. He sounded like a little boy who had peeked at his Christmas present early and saw that he had gotten just what he wanted. "It's my tomb-in-waiting. Isn't it crazy?"

"It is, kind of." *Totally crazy*, thought Crush. Just then he saw something move behind the pyramid. In the gathering dusk, he was on guard, ready for anything. He peered around the tomb to see a woman, head covered in a long scarf, kneeling as if in prayer before Adam Udell's empty mausoleum. He assumed she'd misidentified it for the burial place of a loved one. Should he interrupt her reverie to tell her, or give her the peace she seemed to crave?

Adam didn't ask himself such questions. He walked up and planted himself right in front of her. "As long as you're on your knees, do you want to make yourself useful?" he asked.

The woman lifted her head and Crush could see it was Rachel. "You're late. And do you have to be so crass?"

"It's my way."

She glanced over at Crush. "Hey, Crush. Have you

heard from my dad? He was supposed to meet me for lunch."

Crush shook his head.

"Your father's here? I'd love to see him again. He's a real piece of work," Adam said.

"Later," Rachel said. "Can't you see I'm in mourning for a great film director?"

"I'm great?"

"You were great. Before you started making shit like *The Rage Machine* movies."

"You gotta pay the bills. But you'll be Sancho Panza in my *Don Quixote*."

"Not Dulcinea?"

"Dulcinea's a whore."

"I've played a whore."

"Not anymore. You're a virgin now."

"I am?"

"You're a virgin to me." He brought her to her feet in front of him. "You're pure and untouched."

"Is that right?"

"You know, I'm afraid to kiss you," Adam said.

Crush was starting to feel like a fifth wheel here.

"You are?" Rachel asked him.

"I'm afraid if I kiss you, I'll kiss you like I kiss all the others. It'll ruin it. I wish I were a virgin, too. Never been kissed. So I could kiss you for the first time."

"Try it and see," Rachel said, raising her face to his, offering her lips.

"No," Adam said, "not yet." He led her around to the brass door. Crush could now read what was engraved on it. UDELL. "Do you want to see inside?"

"You want to kiss me in there?" Rachel asked. Crush couldn't tell if she was delighted or appalled.

"Yes."

"Is this your version of Netflix and Chill? 'Cause it's pretty weird."

"Don't joke about it," he said. "I'm offering you my heart here." Adam turned to Crush and said, "Keep an eye out. We'll only be a little while."

Adam pulled an old-fashioned lever-lock key from his pocket and fitted it into the keyhole at the brass door. He swung the door open. "Come on, Rachel," he said. "Let's taste eternity."

"Groovy," she said. And they walked in.

The sun was setting and the shadows lengthened on the ground and reached up to touch Adam's tomb. Crush wondered how long they'd stay in there, what they were doing, and how much of it they were doing. He wondered, too, what exactly he was supposed to be doing out here. "Keep an eye out," Adam had said. For whom? Paparazzi? Stalkers? Polly? Was he a bodyguard or a wingman?

Crush took his sentry pose, relaxed but poised to strike at any sound that seemed out of place. The shadows crept up the sides of the houses of the dead. *What was the name for the darkest part of a shadow again?* he wondered. The umbra? Zerbe would know. He went through crossword puzzles like popcorn at the movies.

Minutes passed. He wondered what was going on in the pyramid. Was Rachel making her move now? Was she changing her strategy? Was she deciding to claim him as her own?

He heard a rattling sound. From behind the mausoleum on his right. Then a footfall on the gravel walkway. This was a public space, Crush told himself. No reason to assume that a visitor was a threat. Still, he tensed as he craned his neck to look. He heard the snap of a camera shutter. He saw a fat man lying in the path, pointing a camera at Adam's tomb. He had a cast on his leg and his right hand was bandaged.

It was Rachel's very own stalker, Brandon Renbourn. Crush hadn't heard him approaching. Had he been here all along, waiting? Crush walked over and tapped him on the shoulder. Brandon tried to scramble away, but Crush caught him by the collar.

"I thought we talked about this," Crush said. "You weren't supposed to do this anymore."

"Didn't she tell you?"

"Tell me what?"

"She said it was okay."

"No, she didn't, Brandon."

"She did. She texted me."

"I'm going to have to hurt you. You know that."

"Ask her. She wants me here. It was all just a misunderstanding. She loves me."

Crush bent to pick Brandon up. He let his guard down, just for a second, thinking this was the intruder he had to worry about. He heard the sound of someone behind him and turned a second too late. Something hard struck him on the top of his head and he fell to the ground.

Instinct took over. Hitting the ground, Crush rolled and pushed himself up from the gravel, the blow still ringing in his skull, and sprang to his feet. Blood flowed from the wound on his head into his eye, partially blinding him, but he could just make out the figure in front of him, raising something over his head. Crush raised his left arm to block the blow and punched with his right, in the direction of the man's throat.

The man dodged the attack and grabbed Crush's hand, throwing him off balance. Stunned as he was, Crush still reacted with the strategy of a born fighter. He let the attacker's move carry him forward, all the way past the man and onto the grass beyond. Falling to the ground, he did a roll and ended up on his feet, outside of his attacker's reach. Even in the gathering gloom, he could see that the man was smiling at him, hefting a heavy length of lead pipe in his hands.

"Mr. Emmerich sends his regards," the man said.

Crush was wiping the blood from his eyes when he remembered. It had been three years since their altercation in the Million Dollar Theatre, but it came back to him like it was yesterday.

"Is that you, Bub?" Crush said. "How've you been?"

"I've been good," he said. "Looking forward to this."

"So that was you I chased out of Adam's hotel room?"

"I'm not saying it was, I'm not saying it wasn't."

"How's the wrist?"

"Healed. It still aches when it rains."

"Sorry about that."

"No worries. I'm going to break your arms," Bub said calmly.

"Are you?"

"Maybe your legs, too. And your skull."

"Do you want me to take notes? In case you forget something?"

"I won't kill you. I'll just damage you forever."

"Sounds like a plan. Listen, are we going to keep talking about this all night or are we going to get down to it?"

Bub stepped forward and swung the pipe at Crush's head. Crush was still woozy but he moved fast enough to evade the blow. He darted behind Bub and punched him hard in the small of his back. Bub grunted but pushed away and spun around, swinging the pipe again. This time Crush was too slow. The pipe connected with his collarbone and he fell to his knees. Bub kicked at his face.

Crush grabbed Bub's foot and yanked, pulling him off balance. Bub stumbled and Crush sprang upright, hammering his fist at Bub's midsection. Bub was wearing some kind of body armor, like a Kevlar vest, so the blows had little impact on him. He certainly came prepared. Bub dropped back against a wrought iron fence and held onto it for support. Crush slugged him in the jaw and then kicked his legs out from under him. He took a deep breath and placed his boot on Bub's throat.

"Are you through?" Crush asked him.

Before Bub could answer, something hard and heavy crashed into the back of Crush's head. He fell forward onto the iron fence.

Moving slowly, like he was trapped in molasses, he tried to push himself off the fence. Again the hard object crashed onto his head, rattling his brain in his skull and forcing him down, forcing the lights to go out and the world to retreat. Blackness and silence swallowed him whole.

CHAPTER THIRTEEN

eing knocked unconscious was not like being asleep. There was no soft rest and regeneration. There were no peaceful dreams. Instead, there was a feeling of being switched off, with electric bursts of the brain trying to switch itself on again. Like a computer that's stuck in a series of glitches, trying to reboot itself.

When Crush opened his eyes, it was still night. He assumed it was the same night. But it could have been another night, twenty years from now. He could have been Rip Van Winkle or Buck Rogers or Fry from *Futurama*. He could have traveled to an unknown and distant era.

Concussion, he thought. He'd felt something sort of like this in Najaf, when an IED had gone off close to him. The medic had told him, "For God's sake, don't go to sleep or you might never wake up."

He looked at his watch. He'd been unconscious for nearly an hour. His right arm felt heavy as if he were holding a rock or a dumbbell. He shifted his eyes to look at what was in his hand. A gun, that's what it was. A pistol. A Beretta, to be exact. The same Beretta that Adam Udell had shown him in the car.

He made it to his feet, a little unsteadily. He fished into his pocket and pulled out his cell phone, switching on the flashlight app. Then he stumbled over to the pyramid and tried the door. It was locked. He hammered on it

and called out, "Rachel!" No answer. Nobody was home.
He hoped.

He noticed that he had a voicemail. It must be important—no one left voicemails in this age of texting. It was
Rachel. She sounded worried. She said they were back at
the hotel and they needed to speak with him. He called
back, but he didn't get an answer.

◎

On the way out of the cemetery, Crush passed the filming
location. Things were in turmoil. Everyone was ready to
shoot. The only problem was that the director and the
leading lady were AWOL.

Byron was surprisingly calm, even though he'd spent
hours getting into his Enforcer makeup and tight-fitting
armor. "I'm not surprised Adam's not here. He listened
to me. He can't bring himself to film this destructive por-
nography." His breath formed a cloud of self-righteous
steam in the night air.

Sterling stood next to him in the dark suit that was
the costume for his role as the delightfully evil Senator.
"But you were willing to don the costume with the machine gun in the arm, weren't you?" he asked.

"I signed a contract," Byron said. "I have a big nut to
make. But I wouldn't have fired the gun. I've decided. No
more killing."

"Where does that leave me?" Sterling asked. "I've got
a dramatic death scene coming up. Are you going to take
that away from me?"

"It will involve some rewrites, I don't deny that.
That's probably what Adam is doing now."

Polly came up to them looking distraught. "Sterling,

have you seen him?" Crush could tell she wasn't just worried about the picture.

"No, I haven't."

"Rachel called me," Crush said. "She said they're back at the hotel."

"What are they doing there?" Polly asked. "He's not answering my calls. The last time anybody saw him, he was walking off through the cemetery. With you." She looked more closely at him. "What the hell happened to you?" She was the first one to notice the damage to Crush's face.

"Yeah, he showed me his tomb," he said.

"He likes to show that off. What then?"

He pulled Polly aside to a more private spot in this most public place. "Rachel met us there."

"Okay."

"They went into the crypt. While I stood guard."

"Kinky. Even for Adam. Are they still there?"

"No." He told her that he'd seen Brandon and Bub. That he was hit on the head and knocked unconscious. "When I came to, they were gone."

"We should go back to the hotel. Maybe he forgot to charge his phone. If they're not there, we'll have to call the police."

Crush nodded. He hoped they were at the hotel. He wasn't too eager to have the police rooting around Adam's pyramid.

Polly called for a car, and Crush went back to the Louisiane with her and Sterling. She hammered on the door of the Faulkner Suite. No answer. She went into her room, came back with the passkey, and opened the door. The suite was empty. The bedroom was empty. Adam's suitcase was gone. His toothbrush and razor were missing from the bathroom.

Crush went over to the Truman Capote Suite. Rachel's luggage was gone, too. Polly stood in the doorway. "This isn't good," she said.

"The two of them probably ran off somewhere," Sterling said. "Call the front desk. See if they checked out."

Polly picked up the room phone. She talked for a few minutes, then hung up and put her head in her hands.

"What is it, Polly?" Sterling asked.

"He checked out," she whispered.

"I told you," Sterling said.

"You don't understand," Polly went on, her voice a little more steady. "He checked us *all* out. The whole cast and crew."

"Can he do that?"

"It doesn't matter whether he can or can't. He did it," she said. "God, I was actually worried about him. I actually worried about that asshole." She started to cry. "It's finally happening. I knew he'd do this one day. I knew he'd just walk away. He's cutting me off."

Sterling paced the room. "Cutting *you* off? What about the rest of us? What about the movie? A director never just walks out on a film. It's unheard of. Unless he's going crazy. Or is too drunk to care."

Polly's cell phone chirped. Quickly, she pulled it out and read a text. She stared at it for a moment and threw the phone across the room. "That cocksucking motherfucker!"

"Is that Adam?" Sterling asked.

"Yes! It's that motherfucking cocksucking son of a bitch!" She caught her breath. "He fired me!"

"Fired you?" Sterling asked. "Fired you from what?"

She walked across the room and picked up the phone

and shook it. "The fucking bastard! He says he no longer thinks I'm a good fit for editing his films. A good fit! Fit this up your fucking asshole, you..."

She sagged, sorrow beginning to replace her fury. "Adam," she whispered. "I love you. Don't you know that?"

Sterling gave her a hug. He took her phone and looked at it. "It's from Adam's phone, all right. But we don't know if he sent it."

"Oh, he sent it, all right," she said. "Nobody could capture that total disregard for human feeling so perfectly."

Then Sterling's phone chimed and it was his turn to read a text. He looked up at them, embarrassed. "It's Adam. He wants me to go to the Hotel Monteleone. He says he's setting up a new command post there. We'll start shooting again tomorrow."

Polly didn't look in the least surprised. "You know why he changed hotels? So he wouldn't have to break up with me face to face. When I get back home, he'll have the locks changed at the house. My stuff will be in storage. I'm being frozen out." Polly smiled a sad smile. "But don't worry, Sterling. You're safe for now. You still have the king's favor."

Sterling shook his head. "To hell with that. He can't do this to you. He can't do this to himself. He loves you. He's told me that so many times. You're his muse."

"He's got a new one now," Polly said.

"Fucking idiot," Sterling said.

"Don't rock the boat," Polly said. "You're too old to find another patron."

Sterling walked to the door. "No, I'll tell him what I really think. To his face. I'll tell him he's throwing away the best part of himself."

"It's too late. He's made up his mind. I don't even

know if I want to go back to him."

"Don't say that. I'll straighten him out or I swear to God I'll never talk to him again."

"Really?" Polly sounded dubious.

"Really." The old man hesitated. "Only...he swears he'll help me get another movie made. He's setting up a pitch with Sony."

"I understand," she said.

"It's just that without him, those bastards won't even meet with me. They say I'm too old. Hell, I'm no older than that hack Clint Eastwood. Or Jean-Luc Godard. If they can direct pictures, why can't I?"

"Sterling, it's okay," she said gently.

"You understand, don't you?" Sterling asked Crush. "It's such a killer project. It'll put me back on the A-list. A science-fiction version of *Don Quixote*—doesn't that sound great?"

"Yeah," Crush said, lying back on the sofa. "I can see it now. The windmills will be space stations."

"That's right!" He started out the door, then stopped and turned back. "But I'll talk to him. I'll tell him he's acting crazy."

"Don't bother. It's done. I've been replaced."

Sterling walked out.

Polly looked around the room. "I don't know what to do now."

"You're better off," Crush said.

"I know, but...for twenty years he's been my life. I don't know who I am without him."

"You're you."

"Very funny." She shook her head, sadly. "She won. I underestimated the clever bitch." She paced rapidly about the room. Then, as if to do something, anything, she stopped to examine the wound on Crush's head. "Jesus, that looks bad. You should get to a hospital."

"I don't do hospitals."

"That's stupid. You must have a concussion."

"I'm fine."

Polly got on her phone and called Dr. ten Berge. In a few minutes the doctor's stern eyes were examining Crush's head wounds and checking his pupils. She turned off her penlight. "You have a concussion."

"I'll walk it off," he said. Another cell phone vibrated and it took Crush a moment to realize it was his. He took it out and read the text.

"Yr services r no longer needed – A Udell"

CHAPTER FOURTEEN

In the end, Polly and Crush were the only two people Adam fired. While everyone else moved to the Monteleone, the two of them left the French Quarter and checked into the Best Western on less fashionable St. Charles Avenue. Crush went into his room and collapsed on the bed. His brain was still sluggish. Dr. ten Berge had bandaged his head and given him a bottle of painkillers, which he left in the room at the Louisiane. He wasn't about to start popping pills. He had his sobriety to think about.

He got up, took the Beretta out of his jacket pocket, and put it in the hotel safe. He took a long shower, and when he was drying off, his cell phone rang. It was Polly. "Hey. Did I wake you?"

"Not yet," he said.

"I tried to call some of my friends in the production to find out what's going on. No one would tell me anything. Most of them didn't even answer my call. He's closed the iron door on me," she said with a wry laugh. "Do you recognize that line?"

Crush said he didn't.

"It's from the first movie Adam and I ever went to together, at a UCLA film class. *Twentieth Century* with John Barrymore and Carole Lombard. A classic screwball comedy. We laughed and laughed. Barrymore played a megalomaniac director with a God complex. I didn't know how realistic it was."

"Get some sleep, Polly."

"I don't suppose you want to come by here. I'm just next door."

"I don't think that would be a good idea."

"Or I could come by there."

"Go to sleep, Polly."

"I'm not paying you anymore. We're both unemployed. There's no reason we can't drown our sorrows in each other."

"You're in a vulnerable condition right now, Polly, and I don't want to..."

"Take advantage of me? Trust me, I *want* to be taken advantage of. All over. I need it."

"Sleep."

"Don't be such a gentleman, Rush. If you turn me down, I'll just go down to the hotel bar and find a hookup."

"This hotel doesn't have a bar." He hung up. Polly was a very attractive woman, and Crush felt a pang of regret that he'd turned her down. He was still feeling woozy, but he imagined he'd have risen to the occasion, as it were. But no matter how he tried to justify it, he knew she wasn't thinking straight. And if he'd learned anything in his thirty-plus years, it was to not take a woman to bed unless she had all her faculties in good working order. Otherwise it got confusing. Hell, it got confusing anyway, but that was a sure recipe for disaster.

He lay in bed and tried to meditate, but his brain was still unruly. He turned on the TV and watched a stand-up comedian who thought he was funny but wasn't until he fell asleep.

A rapid knocking on the hotel door awakened him. He checked his watch. It was three-fifteen in the morning.

He got up, pulled on his pants, went to the door, and opened it.

Polly stood in the hallway, nude, staring at him with hungry eyes. Her body was lean and lanky, and the nipples on her tiny breasts were jutting out at him, as if in anger. "I have some issues I need to work through," she said.

She kissed him fiercely. Kissing her back, he wrapped his arms around her. She pushed him into the room, onto the bed, biting him, digging her fingers into his flesh.

He'd tried to do the right thing, but sometimes a good disaster was hard to avoid.

◎

His cell phone rang at seven a.m. He woke up, feeling sore in unexpected places. Polly had left after a couple of hours, saying she didn't want to wake up next to Crush, since she was going to have to get used to waking up alone. He picked up his phone, thinking it was Polly calling him. It was Rachel's number.

He let it ring a few times, then answered.

"Hey, Crush. Have you heard from my dad?" Just that. No "sorry about leaving you unconscious in a graveyard" or anything.

"No, I haven't."

"I was supposed to meet him yesterday. And I've called all his numbers, even his 'red alert' number. He hasn't called me back. I'm worried."

Crush didn't ask where she was supposed to meet Lloyd. That could wait. "Do you need help?"

"Yes. I want to go to his motel. But I don't want to go alone."

"And Adam?"

"He's busy rewriting the script."

"All right. I'll be over in ten minutes."

He got dressed and sent a text to Polly saying he'd be back before noon. He hopped a streetcar to the French Quarter and walked the rest of the way. It was cooler today, with a brisk breeze blowing, and Rachel was waiting out in front of the Monteleone wrapped up in a hoodie like a child who'd been left alone in a crowd. Crush walked up and she nodded toward a black sedan. They got in back and the driver pulled out. It was a studio transportation car. Even in this crisis, Rachel was still a movie star.

She got in the car quickly without even looking at him. "Why don't you want to go alone?" Crush asked as the car pulled out. She looked up at him and noticed the damage. "Jesus, you look like hell. What happened?"

"That's what I was going to ask you," he said. "What happened in Cemetery Number Four last night? After you started playing grab-ass in Adam's crypt."

"We were fooling around. Just a little bit. Just enough to keep him interested. You were out keeping watch. We heard a scuffling outside. Adam went out to see what it was."

"What did you do?"

"I stayed in the tomb. Then I saw Brandon. He just walked up to the crypt and said hello. I thought you were supposed to be protecting me from him."

"I was busy."

"I think Brandon had a knife."

"You think?"

"It was dark. I was in a fucking tomb, remember? Then Adam showed up behind him. He pulled him out and socked him."

"Socked?"

"Punched. Hit. Slugged. You know, what I mean."

"What did Brandon do?"

"I don't know. Fell down? Ran away? Adam came in, grabbed me, and we ran off. All the way back to the hotel. So Adam saved me. While you were off doing God knows what."

"And that's it?"

"No. Adam realized then that he loved me. He also realized that he couldn't keep making this picture this way. He had to postpone shooting until he could do a major rewrite."

"And he fired Polly?"

"He had to. She was a part of his old life."

"And he fired me?"

"You let us down."

"So you won. He's going to marry you. You get all his stuff."

"I know you won't believe this, but I don't care about that. I mean, I'm glad that I have it. I'm glad I can get Lustig off my back. But that's not what's important. What's important is that I'm going to marry Adam. I love him."

"This is me you're talking to. You don't have to pretend."

"I know. But I'm not pretending."

"You fell for your mark? Just like in the movies?"

"It's kind of funny, isn't it?"

"And sudden. When did you realize you were in love with him?"

"I guess it was when I was in his crypt. Up until then I'd just been playing a part. But when I saw him tackle

Brandon, when I realized what I meant to him... I don't know. My heart just melted."

"Did it? Did it melt?"

"I know it sounds stupid. But love is kind of stupid, isn't it?"

They pulled up to the Motel Six. Rachel gripped his arm when she saw it: yellow police tape cordoning off the parking lot. There was a cop car parked by the front office.

"Stay here," Crush said as the sedan pulled up.

"To hell with that," she said, jumping from the car before it had even stopped.

"Wait here," Crush told the driver, leaping out to join her as she ran. She crouched under the caution tape, heading for Room 103. She stopped in front of the open door. Crush joined her and looked in.

Two white uniformed policemen and a black woman in a sharp business suit were searching the room.

"I'm afraid you have to stand back, ma'am," one of the unis said. "This is a crime scene."

"Fuck that," Rachel replied.

The other uni looked up at her. "Hey. Aren't you Rachel Strayhorn?"

"Fuck that, too," she said. "This is my father's room."

That was when the woman took notice of them. "Hello, ma'am, I'm Lieutenant Savoy of the NOPD," she said as she took a copy of a driver's license out of her pocket. "Do you know this man?"

The driver's license photograph was of Lloyd Fury, although the name on the license was George Kaplan.

"Yes, that's my father."

"Your father is George Kaplan?" the lieutenant asked.

"No, my father is Lloyd Fury, but that's his picture."

"What's your name, ma'am?"

"My name is Rachel Fury. But I go by Strayhorn."

"I knew it," the second cop said. "You were great in that *Winter* movie."

"What's going on?" Crush asked.

"Miss Fury," the lieutenant said, "I'm sorry to have to tell you, but your father is dead."

Rachel looked like she'd been struck. "How?"

"He was shot."

"Where?"

"Outside. Behind the ice machine."

Rachel nodded. "So he was taking cover. He knew they were after him."

"Knew *who* was after him, ma'am?"

"Whoever shot him. And stop calling me ma'am."

"Would you be willing to come down to the station? To identify the body?"

"I guess I have to," Rachel said. "What are you going to do with his stuff?"

"It's evidence, Miss Fury."

"Even that?" she said, pointing to a sack of glass eyes on the bed.

"I'm afraid so."

"We'll wait outside," Rachel said.

"Miss Fury," Savoy said as Rachel walked out, "why did he have so many glass eyes?"

"He used to lose them," she said. "For a living."

◉

They were in the police station next to the Café Lafitte, where Lloyd had eaten beignets just the day before. Walking down the dank hallway toward the morgue, Rachel said to Crush, "I always knew I'd be doing this someday. Going to identify his body."

Crush squeezed her hand, like the brother he never was. Lieutenant Savoy stood beside a gurney in the chilly, dimly lit morgue. They approached a body covered in a white sheet. Crush held Rachel's hand as the attendant lifted the sheet. Rachel started crying, blubbering, howling with sorrow. If it had been anyone else's body on that gurney, top of the head blown off, empty eye socket staring, Crush would have thought she was putting on a pretty good act. But this was her father, and he knew the grief was real.

"Can you identify him?" Savoy asked.

"It's Lloyd Fury," Crush answered. Rachel just kept on crying. She was still wiping her eyes and gasping for breath when Savoy took them to a little room with a large mirror across one wall to "answer just a few questions."

"Would you excuse us?" Savoy asked Crush.

"Let him stay," Rachel said, catching her breath. "I don't want to be alone here."

"All right," Savoy said, pulling up a chair and offering a box of Kleenex.

"Can they hear us?" Rachel asked, blowing her nose.

"Who?" Savoy asked.

"The people behind the mirror. I don't want to have to do this twice." She seemed to have collected her thoughts.

"One time will be enough," the lieutenant said. "Why did your father have so many different IDs in so many different names?"

"He was a con man."

"Was he here on a con?"

"He was here visiting me. But he may have been moonlighting, I suppose."

"You weren't aware of any criminal activities?"

"No."

"Do you know of anyone who would have a motive to kill him?"

Rachel sighed. "My father was a low-level grifter. I'm not proud of that fact, but I'm not ashamed of it, either. He ripped off a lot of people over a lot of years. Any of them might have wanted him dead, but I don't know of anyone in particular in New Orleans. He'd only been here a day."

Savoy looked at Crush. "And what is your involvement in this?"

"He's my bodyguard," Rachel said.

Her eyes darted back to Rachel. "You need a bodyguard?"

"I'm an actress. Maybe you've heard of me."

"I haven't actually. I don't get to the movies much. But I understand you're famous."

"Yes. And stalkers go with the territory. An occupational hazard."

"Is it possible that one of these stalkers could have targeted your father?"

Rachel reacted with sharp intake of breath. She turned to Crush, "You don't think so?"

"It's possible," Crush said. "But this particular stalker prefers to use a knife."

"And who is this?" Savoy asked.

"Brandon Renbourn," Crush went on. "Miss Fury has a restraining order against him. She saw him last night."

"Where?"

"At the film shoot."

"What time?"

"Around five-thirty or six."

"That would have been long after your father was killed. Did he say anything to you?"

Rachel shook her head. "We avoided him."

"Do you have a picture of him?"

"I can get you one."

"We'll put out a BOLO on him. Do you consider him dangerous?"

"I consider him crazy," Rachel said.

CHAPTER FIFTEEN

The production car had waited for them at the police station. The Hotel Monteleone wasn't very far away, but it was cold and Rachel was tired, so she didn't want to walk.

"Who do you think shot him, Rachel?" Crush asked.

"I have no idea."

"It wasn't Brandon, you know that. Tell me about Bub. What was he doing there?"

"I don't know any Bub."

"Whatever his real name is then. Mr. Emmerich's soldier. You know him. You tried to palm off the fake Letters of Transit to him three years ago."

"You mean Meier Lustig's man?"

"If you say so. I saw him in the cemetery last night. Just before I got bashed on the head."

"You think Lustig was behind this?"

Crush took Rachel by the arms and turned her to look at him. "Cut the bullshit, Rachel. Your father's dead. There's more at stake here than a goddamned con. Tell me the truth."

Rachel looked at him. Her eyes started to tear up. But she could do that at the drop of a hat. She spoke to the driver. "Stop. Let us out here."

The driver pulled over and they got out. They were only a few blocks from the hotel. The crowd bustled around them, and Crush knew they couldn't be overheard here. Rachel ignored the cold weather and started talking as soon as her feet hit the pavement. "His name is Eric Gordon, but Lustig called him Bub."

"How is Meier Lustig involved with this?"

"I have to go back three or four years. To the beginning of this goddamn con."

"I'm listening."

"All right. Some of this you know, some of this you've probably guessed. My father was based in Los Angeles then, running scams in Hollywood. Stuff to do with show business collectibles. He heard that Meier Lustig was a nut for old movie memorabilia. Especially anything to do with *Casablanca*. He also heard that Adam Udell had the Letters of Transit from that movie. Adam was out of the country, so he figured we could steal them and sell them to Lustig. Then I thought, why not make copies and sell them to a bunch of people? We could return the real ones to Adam's house, so no one would be the wiser."

"I can't believe you really thought it was a good idea to pull a con on Meier Lustig."

"You know I love a challenge. So we broke into Adam's house, stole the letters, and made copies. But it all fell apart pretty fast. Lustig demanded we get the rest of Adam's collection. He'd seen it, evidently. He had to have all of it."

"Did you know that Lustig and Adam were acquainted with each other?"

"I didn't then. But once I got close to Adam, I found out that Lustig was obsessed with him. He wanted to destroy him. I don't know why."

"I might, but go on."

"Lustig assigned Bub to keep an eye on us. To make

sure we were making progress."

"And he followed you to the cemetery?"

"He might have."

"I don't know if I believe you."

"Why would I lie?"

"Because you're so used to it. I saw him in the grave-yard. Right after I spotted Brandon. We fought."

She gestured to Crush's head. "I'm sorry he hurt you."

"Oh, he didn't do this. Do you think Bub could have killed your father?"

"No. Bub is a soldier. He only does what Lustig tells him to do, and Lustig wanted my father alive to finish the job."

"How well did your father know Adam?"

"They were drinking buddies. Adam loves colorful characters. My father filled that bill."

"I need to talk to Adam."

"I don't know if I can disturb him. He's working on the script."

"Isn't figuring out who killed your father more impor-tant to him than a movie?"

"You don't know show business people very well, do you?"

They'd made it to the Monteleone, a big Beaux Arts edifice on the outer edge of the French Quarter. While walking through the lobby to the elevator, Rachel called Adam on her cell phone to tell him they were coming. "He's not answering. Wait here while I see how he is. We don't want to burst in on him while he's writing."

"Why not?"

"Sometimes he's naked and watching German dungeon porn. It fuels his muse."

Crush didn't want to walk in on that, so he waited in

the lobby while she went up. Glancing into the bar he saw Sterling sitting there nursing a tumbler full of amber liquid. The bar was round and decorated like a carousel. At first he thought it was an optical illusion, but the bar was actually turning slowly around, like a drunkards' merry-go-round.

Crush walked over and climbed onto the stool next to Sterling.

"Hey," he said.

"Hey yourself," Sterling replied. "Do you like the ride? I do. It makes you feel drunk even before you've started drinking."

"Yeah. It's a little early for bourbon, isn't it?" Crush asked.

"Early, late," Sterling said, "what difference does it make?" He was slurring his words a little, so this evidently was not his first drink.

"Something bothering you?"

"Aside from the fact that I can't get hard even if I take five Viagras? I'm old, that's what's bothering me. I'm used up. I should have died in 1995. That was my last good year."

Crush ordered a cranberry juice from the bartender. Sterling snorted. "Why don't you have a real drink?"

"Because I'm an alcoholic, remember?"

"How can you be an alcoholic if you don't drink? That's like being a vegetarian who only eats meat."

"What's bothering you?"

They were gliding past the front windows. Sterling gave a little wave to passersby on the street and then looked back into his empty glass. "I tried to tell him. I actually got up the nerve to tell Adam he was crazy. For dumping Polly."

"How'd it go?"

"I got two words out before he fired me. And he didn't just fire me. He said he was taking my *Don Quixote* idea for himself. Said I was too old to do it justice."

"Can he do that?"

"He can do whatever he wants. He's Adam Udell." He shook the ice in his glass and tried for another swallow. "For now."

"For now?"

"As long as his movies make money. As long as he doesn't piss the studios off. Remember Michael Cimino?"

"No."

"Neither does anybody else. Adam's doing it now. He's going off the deep end."

"How so?"

"He's locked himself in his suite. He's not making his movie. Worse yet, he's rewriting it. He showed me the pages. He's ruining it. Taking out all the action. Making a plea for peace, for God's sake."

"Peace is bad?"

"Peace is fine. In its place. But it's not box office. It's not what people want from *The Rage Machine*. It's not what people want from Adam Udell." He finished his drink. "Mark my words, his days are numbered."

"What's pushing him over the edge?"

Sterling shrugged. "Success? It's a cruel mistress."

"Did he say anything about what happened last night in the cemetery?" Crush asked.

"He just said he was a changed man. That he couldn't go back to being the Adam Udell they want him to be. Trust me, when he shows studio executives those new pages, they'll be on the plane in thirty seconds to shut the production down and hire a new director. I wish I could be there to see it."

Crush's cell phone vibrated. He read the text from Rachel. *Adam will see you for dinner.* He put the phone away.

"Is that from Rachel?" Sterling asked.

"Yep."

"How is she?" Sterling asked.

"Her father's dead."

"Lloyd?" He shook his head in disbelief. "I thought he'd outlive me. What was it? His heart?"

"His head. He got a bullet in it."

"You're shitting me. Who did it?"

"We don't know."

"I liked Lloyd," Sterling said. "He had great stories. He lived a life." Sterling raised his empty glass. "To Lloyd."

It was only at that moment that Crush really accepted that Lloyd was gone from the earth. He was a con man and liar and only out for himself, but he was the closest thing to a father that Crush had ever known. He raised his glass of cranberry juice and clinked. "To Lloyd."

They sat in silence for a moment.

"What are you going to do now?" Crush asked.

"I don't really know," Sterling said. "I'd hire a whore but I couldn't do anything with her except listen to her talk, and I'm not masochist enough for that. I guess I'll just sit here and drink myself to death. That's not as easy as it sounds."

"You want to go back to my hotel? Polly's there."

Sterling cocked an eye toward him. "She is, huh? Nice." He chuckled. "I'm glad you were able to soften the blow for her."

"It's not like that," Crush said.

"Then what is it like?"

Crush couldn't quite answer that question.

"Oh, brother," Sterling said as he watched Crush hesitate. "Don't tell me you're falling for her. That one is *very* complicated. If there's one thing I've learned over the years it's that complicated women are too complicated."

Crush checked his watch. It was one-thirty in the afternoon. He'd told Polly he'd be back by noon. He thought of calling her but decided he'd walk back to the hotel and see if she was still there. He climbed off the carousel and gave Sterling a salute. He'd grown fond of the old guy.

He walked to the Best Western, wrapping his jacket tightly around himself to keep out the chill. Back at the hotel, he knocked on Polly's door and she answered. "You *did* come back," she said. "I thought maybe I'd scared you off."

"It takes a lot more than that to scare me," he said.

They paused in the doorway, both wondering if they should kiss. Kissing now, the first time they saw each other after last night, that would say something. That would say they were in some kind of relationship. Not kissing, that would say that last night was a one-shot deal, born of a broken heart and broken head.

He stepped around her and walked into the room.

"What did you do today?" she asked him.

"Walked around." He was about to tell her the story when she cut him off.

"Cool. Me, I slept late and started reading *Anna Karenina.*" She gestured to her Kindle. "I haven't read it since the last time somebody dumped me. Back in college. It's a whole different book now. When you're over forty Levin becomes the main character." She glanced at him as if she were afraid she had offended him. "But I don't imagine you've read that."

"Why? Russian books have too many big words for me?"

Now she looked sure that she'd offended him. "No, I just—"

"I'm kidding," he said. "Actually I haven't read it. But it's on my sensei's list of books I should know. Right after *Crime and Punishment* and *1984.*"

"How many books are on the list?"

"Five hundred."

"He must be a hard taskmaster."

"She is." He wanted to sit down, but the only places to sit were the desk chair and the bed. If he sat on the chair, she'd have to sit on the bed. If he sat on the bed, she might join him. He remained standing.

"I'd like to meet her, Caleb," Polly said. She called him by his first name. The only other people who did that were Zerbe and Gail. Rush didn't know how he felt about that.

"Her name is Catherine Gail. She saved my life. Taught me how to channel my anger and..." He was cut off mid-sentence by her kiss. It was a softer kiss than the ones she'd given him last night. Those had been angry and devouring. This was a tender, inviting kiss. Her arms were around him, and he found himself kissing her with equal tenderness.

"Are you sure about this?" he murmured.

She gave a little laugh. "You didn't ask that last night."

"You didn't give me the chance."

"I'm sure," she said. Her eyes were wide as she looked at him. "It's the only thing I *am* sure of right now."

They moved to the bed and took their time, exploring each other's bodies with delicate fascination. Time seemed to pause, to be held in place. Forgetting all his troubles, he was lost in the flow of just being. He had no idea whether they were going at it for fifteen minutes or fifteen hours. When they were still, they lay with their arms entwined, their breathing quiet and calm as if they'd had their first good night's sleep in weeks.

"I better not make a habit of that," she said, her head resting on his chest.

"Why not?" he asked, tracing his fingers on her skin.

"I could get hooked," she said. "Tell me about your day. What happened on your walk?"

"Nothing much."

"No." She ran her finger along the scar on his head. "Talk to me. If we're quiet I'll have nothing to think about except how this can't possibly go anywhere."

"Why does it have to go anywhere?"

"See, you're thinking about it, too."

So he told her what had happened that day. He told her about going to the motel with Rachel and finding out that her father had been killed. About going to the morgue to identify the body.

"That's awful," Polly said.

Then he told her he was going to talk to Adam that night. Polly didn't take it too well. She plucked her e-cigarette off the bedside table and started to vape.

"So you're going to talk to Adam. I don't like that. He'll get you in his orbit again. I thought you were out of it, Crush." So he was Crush again.

"I don't care about Adam Udell," Crush said. "I care about Lloyd. I have to find out who killed him."

"From what I saw of Lloyd, you're well rid of him."

"You didn't like him?"

"Well, I didn't trust him. Did you?"

"Not particularly. But I didn't want to see him dead."

She brushed the hair from her eyes. "I didn't kill him, if that's what you're thinking."

"I wasn't thinking that."

"Weren't you?" She sat up straight, naked and angry, ready to pounce.

"Okay, it crossed my mind. But I doubt that you'd use a gun to kill a man."

"What would I use?"

"Your bare hands."

She blew a cloud of electronic smoke at him. "Damn straight. What difference does it make who did it anyway? It was bound to happen. Lloyd and Rachel and Adam, they're all bad news. Those people will do nothing but suck you into their vortex of disaster." She paused. "That would be a good title for a movie. *Vortex of Disaster*. Maybe I'll go home and write it. Not that I have a home."

"You can stay at my place. My brother would be happy to have company."

"Will you come back with me?"

"Not right now. I need to see this through."

"Then fuck you very much, Crush." She got up and went into the bathroom. He heard the shower running. Looking up at the ceiling, he tried to recapture the calm feeling of relaxation that had flowed through his body only minutes before, but it was gone. A knock on the door came as a welcome distraction.

"Just a minute," he said as he pulled on his clothes and opened the door. Lieutenant Savoy stood outside with a uniformed officer backing her up.

"Well, hello, Mr. Rush," she said, looking fake-surprised. "I hope I'm not bothering you."

"Not at the moment," he said. "Are you looking for

Polly Coburn?"

"We were looking for you, actually. You didn't answer your door. We thought Miss Coburn might know where you were."

"Well, here I am. What do you want?"

"Just to let you know that we have apprehended Mr. Renbourn. At least we think we have."

"You think?"

"He has no driver's license and he won't talk. We were wondering if you could come down to the station and ID him."

"Fingerprints won't work?"

"That takes time. We can only hold him for a few hours without charging him. Would you mind?"

Something about this didn't sound quite right to Crush, but he thought he'd play along and see where it led. The shower had stopped, so Crush knocked on the bathroom door. "Polly? I'm going out for a while."

"Are you coming back?" she asked.

"If you want me to."

"I think I want you to."

"Then I think I'll be back."

Lieutenant Savoy eyed him. "Did we come at a bad time?"

"You came when you came," Crush said, heading out the door.

"Don't you want to get your jacket? It's chilly outside," Savoy said.

That didn't sound right either but Crush grabbed his jacket and walked out with them. He wanted to see where Savoy was going with this. They rode the elevator down in silence and walked through the lobby out to the waiting squad car. Climbing into the back seat, he found

Rachel inside.

"They nabbed you, too?" she asked, surprised to see him.

"It looks like it."

Savoy climbed into passenger seat up front. "You really need both of us to identify him?" Crush asked.

"I don't want there to be any mistakes," Savoy said.

They pulled out. After they took a few turns, Crush could tell that they weren't heading for the police station. "Where are we going?"

"Just need to make a quick stop first. Hope you don't mind," Savoy said.

"What if we *do* mind?" Rachel asked.

"It'll only be a minute." Savoy didn't turn around. They were in the back of a patrol car, behind a grate, with no handles on the doors. If they weren't under arrest, Crush couldn't tell the difference.

Rachel didn't speak to Crush. Crush didn't speak to Rachel. They knew enough not to talk in front of the police. The squad car drove around the boundaries of the French Quarter until they reached the gates of Cemetery Number Four. They stopped and the cop who was driving got out and opened the rear door.

Crush and Rachel got out of the car and followed as Savoy led the way into the cemetery. The air was brisk and Crush thought he couldn't wait to get back to the heat and smog of Los Angeles. Savoy led them through the tombstones and crypts, walking in the direction of Adam's pyramid. The uniformed officer went along with her, carrying a duffle bag slung over his arm.

The sky was heavy with dark clouds, and it looked like it might pour at any moment. They reached Adam's tomb. "That's quite a thing," Savoy said. "Have you seen this before?"

Crush knew to stick as close to the truth as possible. "Yeah," he said. "Adam brought me here yesterday."

"Adam Udell?"

"Yes," Rachel said. "That's his mausoleum."

"So I've heard," the Lieutenant said. "And you were here, too?"

"Why do you want to know?" Rachel asked.

"Because...we're the police," Savoy said. "We like to know things."

"Adam brought me here," Crush said.

"And you?" the Lieutenant asked Rachel.

"I came on my own."

"And you just met by coincidence?" Savoy asked.

"It was a date," Rachel said.

"You were having an affair?"

"Not yet. We were building up to one. The journey is half the fun."

"I see. Go on."

Rachel told Savoy how she'd waited to meet Adam and Crush by the gravesite. How they'd gone into the tomb to make out.

"Really?" Savoy said.

"Don't judge," Rachel said. "The heart wants what it wants."

"When did Brandon Renbourn show up?" the Lieutenant asked.

"What makes you think he showed up?" Rachel asked.

"He told me."

"I thought he didn't talk to you," Crush said.

"Oh, I lied about that," Savoy said.

Savoy looked at Crush. "You want to tell me what happened next?"

"Not particularly," Crush said.

"Well, how 'bout if I tell you what Renbourn told *me* and you can correct me anytime the story goes wrong?" Savoy said. "He said he was lying here on the ground, taking pictures. He said you had agreed to it, Miss."

"He's crazy," Rachel said.

"Renbourn said you attacked him, Mr. Rush. Viciously and without provocation. He said he ran off and hid. He said he was terrified."

"I can be pretty terrifying," Crush said.

Savoy turned to Rachel now. "Do you have the key to that door?" she asked, pointing to the pyramid.

"No," she said. "Adam has it."

"And where is Adam Udell? He wasn't at the hotel when we picked you up."

"I told you, he went for a walk. He often does when he's writing."

"We could wait for him to come back," Savoy said, "but I'd really like to look inside there. Wouldn't you, Mr. Rush?"

"Not particularly."

"I could force it open."

"Wouldn't you need a search warrant?" Rachel asked.

"Do you need a search warrant to enter an empty tomb? I don't think so. I could be wrong," Savoy said. "We'll have to look that up. In the meantime," she addressed her man, "I don't believe you've been introduced to Officer Dupuis. Dupuis, get to work."

The uni put down his duffle bag and pulled a crowbar out of it. The door was heavy marble but the lock was rather cheap. After about fifteen minutes of grunting and groaning, he'd pried the door open. Savoy stepped inside and gestured for Crush to join her.

Stepping into the cool marble enclosure, Crush looked around at the empty space. Lieutenant Savoy read an
inscription on the wall. " 'Death and the sun are not to
be looked at steadily.' Is that profound or just common
sense?"

"Why can't it be both?" Crush asked.

"Well, nothing much to see, is there?" the detective
asked, looking around. She rapped her knuckles on the
sarcophagus. "Of course, we could always check in there."

"Why?" Crush asked.

"Why not?" Savoy said. "Go on, open it up. Or do you
refuse?"

Crush shrugged. He lifted the lid on the casket and
looked inside. There was a dead man in there, staring out
at him blankly.

"Well, what do you know about that?" Lieutenant
Savoy said.

CHAPTER SIXTEEN

The dead man in the casket was Bub. He had a bullet hole right below his left eye. Fat lot of good his Kevlar vest had done him.

"You don't look surprised, Mr. Rush," Lieutenant Savoy said.

"Why should I be surprised to find a dead body in a coffin?"

"No reason. Especially since you put it there."

"What makes you say that?"

"Brandon Renbourn said he saw you hide the body in there."

"And you're going to believe him? He also said he got married to Rachel Strayhorn in Vegas. Do you see a ring on her finger?"

"I admit Renbourn isn't the most reliable witness. But the body is right where he said it would be. And you know what else he says?"

"I have a feeling you're going to tell me."

"He says he saw you shoot this man. Care to comment on that?"

"Don't say a word," Rachel said, standing in the doorway.

Crush appreciated Rachel's concern, but she wasn't helping. "I have no recollection of doing any such thing," Crush said.

"Would you mind taking off your jacket, Mr. Rush?" Savoy asked. "And putting it in this evidence bag?"

"Don't do it, Crush," Rachel said.

"Crush?" the lieutenant said. "Is that your street name? I like it. It suits you."

"You want to check the sleeves of my jacket for GSR, is that it?" Gunshot residue could be washed off hands easily enough, but was harder to remove from leather or cloth. Crush took off his jacket and put it in the brown paper bag.

"That's it," Savoy said. "I'm going to have to ask you to come down to the station and answer some questions."

"Are you placing him under arrest?" Rachel asked.

"Let's just say that Mr. Rush is a person of a helluva lot of interest," she said. "But I'm not forgetting about you, Miss. You were here last night. Would you care to contradict Mr. Renbourn's statement? That would be fine. But just remember, lying to the police is called ob-struction of justice, and it's a crime."

Rachel glanced at Crush and looked down at the ground. "I need to talk to my lawyer."

Savoy smiled. "That's what I thought you'd say. It looks like you're on your own, Crush."

◉

"Tell it to me again," Lieutenant Savoy said.

Crush closed his aching eyes. He'd told the story so many times it had begun to become a ritual to him. Even the true parts were sounding like lies to him. "Don't you know it all by now?" he asked. "How 'bout if you say it back to me and I'll tell you what you got wrong."

"Tell it to me again, Crush."

He told it to her again. He left out the parts that incriminated other people. For instance, he didn't tell about meeting Eric years before, when Rachel was trying to pawn off the bogus Letters of Transit. And he didn't talk about Adam and Meier Lustig and his missing mistress. But the rest, he told just how it happened. How he saw Renbourn spying on Rachel. How Eric attacked him. How someone hit him from behind and he woke up with a gun in his hand. That last thing sounded the most like a fabrication.

"Tell it to me again," she said when he was done.

Crush knew she was playing for time. They'd already kept him locked up for a day and a half, far longer than they could lawfully detain him without an arrest. They'd taken his cell phone. They hadn't let him call a lawyer. He could have objected to any number of these abuses, but he knew he was in New Orleans and New Orleans had its own rules. He was just grateful Savoy hadn't gotten a rubber hose or a phone book and started beating him with it. She was a good cop, just doing her job.

"Maybe I can help you," Crush said. "What exactly are you looking for?"

"The truth. Do you really expect me to believe that you can't remember what happened?"

"Not really. But it's the truth."

"You have no idea how the gun got in your hand?"

"No."

"We've searched your hotel room, you know."

"I hope you had a warrant."

"We found a gun. Do you think it's going to turn out to be the gun that shot Eric Gordon?"

"Probably."

"We also found gunshot residue on your jacket sleeve."

"I was afraid you would."

"It would take quite a marksman to hit him in the head like that. Your military record says you scored very high in that area."

"Above average. Better than some, not as good as others. If you're interested, I didn't kill him."

"And that Beretta just magically appeared in your hand?"

"Not magically."

"Next you'll be telling me you were framed."

"It's possible."

"Look, I can see what happened. Brandon Renbourn was stalking Miss Strayhorn. You were her bodyguard. You wanted to protect her. You got into a scuffle. In the confusion, you fired. Unfortunately, you hit the wrong man."

"Bub Gordon. Who just happened to be there?"

"That's right. It's a public place. He was in the wrong place at the wrong time. When you saw what had happened, you panicked. You hid the body where you thought no one would ever find it. At worst it would be manslaughter."

"How many years would I get for that?"

"Fewer than you'd get for first-degree murder. 'Fess up."

"Why don't you tell me something? How is the investigation into the murder of Lloyd Fury going?"

"You want to confess to that instead?"

"Be serious. Did you find any evidence? Fingerprints?"

"Nothing. Just some graffiti scratched on the lid of the ice machine. It may have been left before the shooting."

"What did it say?"

"Two letters: FC. Mean anything to you?"

"Nope."

"Anyway, we don't think the shootings are related."

"Really? Two killings in one day, one Rachel Fury's father, the other in Rachel Fury's presence—and you don't think they're related? What does ballistics tell you?"

"Lloyd Fury was not shot by the same gun that killed Bub Gordon."

"Did Bub have a gun on him?"

"No. What can you tell me about him?" she asked.

"He was a gangster. He belonged to Meier Lustig. Have you heard of him?"

"Sure. What was Bub doing here?"

"I don't know. But he never went anywhere without a gun. Someone must have taken it."

"Who?"

"The same person who put him in the tomb. The same person who killed him."

"Do you think Bub killed Lloyd Fury?"

"It's likely."

"Then I take it back. I don't think you shot Bub accidentally. I think you deliberately killed him to avenge Lloyd Fury's death."

"Now we're getting somewhere," Crush said.

"Then you admit it?"

"No, but at least you're thinking now. You want me to go over it again?"

"No. I have enough. I am arresting you for the murder of Eric 'Bub' Gordon."

Crush sighed. "You really won't let that drop, will you?"

"When I like an idea, I stick with it. You have the right to remain silent..."

◉

Crush was in a windowless jail cell. They'd moved him here from another windowless room five hours ago and left him blessedly alone. He passed the time doing some exercises Gail had been teaching him. They'd been exploring the ancient Indian martial art of *musti-yuddha*, which means "fist combat" in Sanskrit. It was a brutal form of boxing that consisted simply of strikes with the hand at any part of the body. No footwork, no kicking. Just punching your opponent into submission. It was a primitive martial art, one of the first ever recorded, and it was just what Crush needed right now, because the conditioning exercises consisted of toughening his fists by slamming them against a hard surface. Rocks or coconuts were the preferred target, but the cell's cinderblock walls substituted nicely. Punching the wall felt really good right about now. While he hit the wall as hard as he could, he tried to figure out what the hell was going on in Adam Udell's crazy world, and who really had killed Eric Gordon and Lloyd Fury.

He'd struck his fist against the wall seven times when he heard the cell door open and turned to see a guard letting in a well-dressed man with a receding hairline and advancing, bushy eyebrows to make up for the hair loss. He carried a fancy attaché case and looked every inch a high-priced lawyer.

"Hello, Mr. Rush," he said, his voice dripping with an unearned familiarity. "Have you taught that wall a lesson?"

Crush was breathing heavily. "Who are you?"

"I'm Jerome Dembitz. Your lawyer."

"You don't look like a public defender."

"I'm not."

"Then who's paying you?"

"An interested party who wishes to remain anonymous. I want to go over your case."

"Go over it then," Crush said. "No one's stopping you." He slammed his fist into the wall again.

"Let me hear your side of the story."

"Is Adam Udell paying you?"

"My client wishes to remain anonymous."

"I thought I was your client."

"Touché. You are indeed my client."

"Then who's paying you?"

"An interested party who..."

Crush cut him off. "Is it Rachel?"

"We can waste all the time you want. Or I can help you get out of here."

"Or make sure I stay in?"

Dembitz sighed. "I assure you, Mr. Rush, I am an ethical lawyer. No matter who is paying me, the best interest of my client is my only concern."

"Really? Your only one?"

"The police have a great deal of circumstantial evidence against you, Mr. Rush. But it's only circumstantial."

"Don't they have a witness? Isn't that called direct evidence?"

"Somebody's been watching *The Good Wife*. Yes, that is called direct evidence. But only if the witness is unimpeachable. Brandon Renbourn is pretty impeachable. We just need another witness."

"It happened in a cemetery. There are a lot of dead witnesses."

"And two living ones. Adam Udell and Rachel Strayhorn. I need to talk to them. Do you have any idea where they are?"

"So they're not paying you?"

"Do you have any idea where I can find them, Mr. Rush?"

"They're not that hard to locate. They're famous."

"So they have the means to disappear if they wish."

"Have they disappeared?"

"They don't return my calls. I may have to subpoena them."

"Call them as hostile witnesses? I got that from *Perry Mason*."

"You've known Rachel since she was a child, Mr. Rush. If she were to try to hide, where would she go?"

Crush considered. "Who are you working for?"

"Mr. Rush, your bail hearing is about to be held. Cooperate with me and I'll see that it's set at a reasonable amount. If not..."

"Are you working for Meier Lustig?"

"If you can't help me with Rachel Fury, perhaps you can help me locate Polly Coburn."

"Why the hell would you want to talk to her?"

"Mr. Rush, to be honest, my client, who wishes to remain anonymous, is not interested one whit in you. You can rot your life away in prison as far as he is concerned. The person he's interested in is Adam Udell."

"Why?"

"That doesn't concern you. Suffice it to say, my client wants to destroy Adam Udell and everyone and everything he loves. Is that clear enough for you?"

"I think I want a new lawyer."

"Why? Why should you protect Udell? Who do you think put that gun in your hand? Who do you think framed you? Adam Udell is no friend of yours."

"Polly and Rachel are."

"That's their bad luck. All I ask is that you do one

favor for me. If you don't help me, I'll see that bail is set at five hundred thousand dollars. Which is, I think, out of your price range, is it not?"

"Five thousand dollars is out of my price range. What do you want me to do?"

"Deliver Adam Udell to my client."

"The one who wishes to remain anonymous?"

"Exactly. Do you agree?"

"I don't like Adam Udell much. But I'm not a delivery boy. Find him yourself."

"My client could do that. But he'd prefer that you find him. If you won't deliver him, could you at least ask him one question?"

"What's that?"

"Who does he truly love, Polly Coburn or Rachel Fury?"

"Why does your client want to know that?"

"Because he doesn't really want to kill both of them. Just the one that Udell loves the most. However if no further information is forthcoming, my client will have to..."

Crush slammed his fist into the wall just inches from Dembitz's head. The lawyer flinched, cowering as Crush prepared for another blow.

"I think we're done here," Crush said. "Close the cell door on your way out."

Back in Los Angeles, K.C. Zerbe was looking out at MacArthur Park from the window of the loft he shared with Crush on Wilshire Boulevard. Catherine Gail was over for lunch.

"I think the city is getting better, don't you?" he asked Gail. "I really think the whole world's getting better."

"It could be. Since I'm your friend, can I ask you something?"

"Of course."

"Could you put on some pants?"

"Did I forget that again? Damn."

"Some underwear would be nice, too."

"So this is a formal lunch?"

"Humor me."

Zerbe was about to get some clothes when his cell phone rang. "Well, hello, brother! You don't call, you don't write. I was beginning to think you'd dropped off the face of the earth." He listened and nodded a few times. "Okay. I'll tell her. Take care." He ended the call and went to get dressed.

"Was that Rush?" she asked when he returned wearing Batman pajama pants.

"Oh, yeah. He says hi."

"How's he doing?"

"Okay. He's been arrested."

"What for?"

"Murder, I guess. They say he shot somebody."

"Who?"

"He didn't say. He needs you to go bail him out."

"In New Orleans?"

"I guess."

"How much is his bail?"

"Seven hundred thousand dollars."

"I don't have that much."

"I do."

"You do? I thought the Feds took all your money."

"So did they. But I socked some away. For emergencies."

"Can you get hold of it?"

"Sure. Might take a few days. But don't worry. Caleb

would feel good. He pulled out his phone and called Rachel. She didn't answer. He called Polly. Also no answer.

Looking toward the bar, he saw a familiar face.

"Dr. ten Berge," he said, grabbing a seat at the rotating bar. "How are you?"

"I am well," she said. Letting her eyes fall on Gail, who was perching precariously on her stool, she asked, "Who is your lovely friend?"

"This is Catherine Gail. Gail, this is Dr. ten Berge."

"Please call me Alva."

"I'd shake hands, but I'm afraid to let go of the bar," Gail said.

"Yes, it's a landmark of the Vieux Carré," the doctor said. "The Carousel Bar. It provides a lovely panoramic vista of the entire inside of the lobby. What brings you to the Big Easy, my dear?"

"I came to see him," Gail said, pointing to Crush.

"She had to bail me out of jail," Crush said.

"I was wondering where you went off to," the doctor said. "I'm surprised Rachel or Adam didn't see to you. Instead you had to turn to your girlfriend."

"I'm not his girlfriend," Gail said.

"Interesting." The doctor brightened a bit.

"Aren't you going to ask what I was arrested for?" Crush asked.

"I'm not really all that interested in you, Mr. Rush," ten Berge said. "You, on the other hand..."

Gail smiled. "You're moving a little fast, Alva."

"Forgive me, but at my age you have to."

Crush didn't know how old Dr. ten Berge was and didn't really care to ask. "Where is everybody?" he asked. "Did they move to another hotel?"

"They moved back to their old lives. Production was

isn't going anywhere."

◉

Gail was waiting for Crush by a rental car in front of jail. She hadn't dressed warmly enough for this town.

"You look like hell," she said.

"Thanks," Crush replied.

"Let me take you to my hotel. I have a razor there You can shave that five o'clock shadow off your head."

He ran his big hand over the stubble on his head a they got into a blue Ford Focus. "Can you tell I'm going bald?"

"Yes, your secret is out," Gail said. "What's going on, Rush? How'd you get that bandage on your head?"

"It's a long story. I either killed somebody or some-body's trying very hard to make it look like I killed somebody." He told her the whole story, including the friendly visit with Jerome Dembitz.

"Did you tell the lieutenant what he said?" Gail asked.

"Oh, I told her. She didn't believe me. Thought I was making it up to confuse her. It kinda hurt my feelings, to be honest."

"You have strange taste in women."

"What can I say? Lieutenant Savoy intrigues me."

"Where do you want to go?" Gail asked.

"The Best Western on St. Charles."

When they got there, he found that Polly had checke out. And when they went to the Hotel Monteleone, I learned that Rachel had checked out as well. Along wi the rest of the film crew. The desk clerk didn't kno where they'd gone. Crush stood in the middle of t lobby, not sure what to do next. A shower and sha

shut down. Adam Udell is off *The Rage Machine*. Rumor
has it that Rian Johnson is taking over."

"Where'd they go?"

She shrugged. "I don't know. They haven't called me.
I stayed on in the Crescent City because it reminds me
of home."

"Where's home?" Gail asked her.

"Amsterdam. Have you ever been there?"

"I'm afraid I haven't."

"We should go there sometime."

"Amsterdam?"

"Why not? I'm heading back to Los Angeles tonight.
Why don't you let me take you to dinner and tell you
about it?"

"That's tempting," Gail said.

"But I'm afraid we have to talk to my lawyer now,"
Crush said.

The doctor didn't take her eyes off of Gail. "Do you
really have to join him for that?"

"Sadly, yes," Gail said. "He's facing a murder charge."

"Ah, I see. Back in LA then?"

"We'll see," Gail said, jumping off the revolving bar
to follow Crush out.

"*Farvel*, my sweet," ten Berge called over her shoulder.

"I got you out of there just in time," Crush said, once
they were out on the street.

"I don't know," Gail said. "She seemed kind of interesting. And I haven't dated for a while."

"I really *did* get you out of there just in time, didn't I?"

They headed for her car, which was parked a few
blocks away in the Warehouse District. "Where's your
lawyer?"

"I have no idea. Probably in a cave somewhere,

hanging upside down. If I never see him again it'll be fine with me."

"Then where are we going?"

"Back to LA. I have to find Rachel and Polly. They're in danger."

"Didn't your new girlfriend, Lieutenant Savoy, tell you not to leave town?"

"Let her try and catch me."

HOLLYWOOD AND VINE

CHAPTER SEVENTEEN

Crush had to stay off the radar, so they couldn't fly back to Los Angeles. Gail purchased an old VW Golf from a used car lot on Tchoupitoulas Street and they took to the road. Even driving nonstop and pushing the speed limit, the trip took two days. Along the way, Crush repeatedly tried to call Rachel, Adam, Polly, and Sterling, first from his cell phone and then from Gail's. He got no answer from either phone. He left messages and got no calls back. He even emailed and texted them, to no avail. He'd never felt so impotent before.

"They're ghosting you," Zerbe said, over a spotty connection on Gail's phone.

"What does that mean?"

"It's when someone cuts you off from all electronic and online contact."

"What about real contact? Face-to-face contact?"

"That's considered very twentieth century. It's almost never done."

"I'm an old-fashioned guy," Crush said. "And thanks," he added after a pause.

"For what?"

"For the bail money. You'll get it back. Probably."

"No worries. I'm just glad I had it. I wasn't able to find out much, by the way."

"About what?"

"About where Brandon Renbourn is. Remember you asked me."

"Oh, yeah. Well, keep trying. I need to talk to him, too."

"I was able to trace him backwards though. Last year he took a bunch of trips. To New York. To Chicago."

"The usual stalking tour."

"Also he got married six months ago."

"He didn't."

"He did. To someone named Eve Sidwich. In Vegas."

"He told me he married Rachel there."

"Well, maybe she was standing in for Rachel. In Brandon's mind Eve is evidently a pro. She has a record for soliciting."

"I'm sure they'll be very happy."

"Caleb, I have to say it—do you know what you're doing? They're bound to notice you left New Orleans. They're bound to be looking for you."

"I can disappear."

"Really? 'Cause you're a big guy. You stand out, I'm telling you."

"I can blend in. I'm already growing my hair back."

"Oh, that's not a good look for you."

"And I'll grow a beard."

"That's even worse. What's your plan? To be the Avenging Hipster?"

"No. I'm just going to un-ghost some people. Before they're ghosted for good." He ended the call.

"We're passing Palm Springs," Gail said. "Where do you want to go first?"

"Blue Jay Way."

◉

Adam's house was locked up and no one answered the bell. Crush thought of breaking in but decided it could wait. It was nine o'clock on Sunday morning, and he needed a place to stop and regroup. He couldn't go to his loft, obviously, or to Gail's apartment; she'd bailed him out, so they'd look there. He could check into a hotel, but he'd have to use either his credit card or Gail's credit card, and either way they could trace him. He had to go somewhere else.

Tarzana is a bland, depressing section of the San Fernando Valley out past Encino. The streets are studded with midcentury apartment buildings, fast-food joints, nail salons, vape stores, and massage parlors. Bill Ingoll lived in a concrete-block apartment house on Etiwanda Street.

Crush had met Bill on a cloudy day seven years before when Gail had forced him to go to an AA meeting in the old Church of the Brethren on Sixth Street. It hadn't taken then, of course. No one who goes to Alcoholics Anonymous on someone else's command ever stays sober. But the next year, when Crush had hit the proverbial rock bottom, Bill was there. He became Crush's sponsor and helped him get out of the hole he'd dug for himself. Crush didn't go to meetings regularly anymore. That was a bone of contention with Bill, but Crush still kept in touch with him nearly every day. Nearly.

"You haven't been checking in, Crush," was the first thing Bill said as he opened the door.

"I've been busy."

"Unless you've been in the hospital or in jail, there's no excuse."

"I was in jail."

Bill nodded. "You may enter."

Bill Ingoll was a lanky, youthful sixty-four. His spiky gray hair stood up on his head, and the wicked gleam in his eye always made Crush think that if Huckleberry Finn had lived to retirement age he'd look like Bill.

Bill's apartment was small and sparsely furnished. "I've had to downsize," he explained to Gail. "From the downsizing I did before. And the downsizing I did before that. If I live much longer, I'll be downsized to a cardboard box under the freeway." They commiserated for a while about the high cost of living in LA and how the overcrowding and the traffic were making it an almost impossible place to live anymore, but how they couldn't picture living anywhere else. Then Gail headed out to pick up the letters.

"They're in the safe behind the *Yojimbo* poster," Crush said. "Zerbe knows the combination. Just bring them back here when you can. But get some sleep first."

"I'll bring them by here," she said, "then I'll sleep."

Once she was gone, Bill poured some tea and set a cup in front of Crush. "You're in the middle of trouble."

"Yep."

"You want to tell me about it?"

"I would if I could, but I don't understand it myself."

"It's out of your control?"

"Everything's out of my control. Haven't we established that?"

"It's good to hear you say it."

"I have to figure out my strategy. There are two women I need to protect. I don't know where they are, and they hate each other. There's a man who's in danger, too. I don't really like him, but I don't want to see him dead."

"And isn't there a pesky murder charge hanging over your head?"

"That too. It's very irritating. I just can't see spending the rest of my life in prison."

"Really? 'Cause I can."

Crush ignored that. "I don't think the person who framed me is the same one who's threatening Rachel and Polly. I think they're two different people."

"There are two antagonists in the story? Messy." Bill had been a screenwriter before the drinking took over. He was still a screenwriter at heart. "But who's the mastermind behind it all?"

"I don't know. There are possibilities."

"Suspects?"

"If you like. There's an obvious one."

"Well, if this was a movie, I'd say it's never the obvious one. But in real life? Go with the obvious, every time."

◉

Crush took a hot shower, then a cold shower, had some soup, and tried to rest. Then Gail showed up with the letters. "What are they?" Gail asked.

"A prop. From the movie *Casablanca*. They're worth a fortune."

Bill leaned in to take a look. "I'll never understand why people pay good money for movie props. They're just make-believe."

"*Casablanca*? Is that the one where Bogart was looking for the statue of a black bird?" Gail asked.

"No," Bill said, "that's *The Maltese Falcon*."

"Is it the one where he was going down some river in Africa with an old lady?"

"That's *The African Queen*. I'll make you a list."

While they were discussing this, Crush tried Sterling Bolsinger's number on Gail's phone one more time. To his surprise, Sterling answered. "Sterling, this is Rush. I'm calling from a friend's phone."

"Rush! I thought you were arrested? Did they let you go?"

"It's a long story. Why haven't you been answering your phone?"

"It's a long story, too."

"Where are you now?"

Sterling said he was closing up his house on Mulholland Drive and moving to an apartment in Hollywood. "1500 Vine Street, apartment 1012. Be there in an hour."

Crush ended the call and asked Bill if he could borrow his car. "I'll return it with a full tank of gas."

"We both know I'll be lucky if you return it at all," Bill said, dropping the keys into Crush's hand.

For years, Hollywood Boulevard was a rundown, sleazy collection of tattoo parlors, souvenir and T-shirt shops, and dilapidated movie palaces that had been split into three or four tiny screening rooms that showed either Italian zombie films or X-rated parody films that were probably better than the films they were making fun of. That was the Hollywood Crush had grown up with, the Hollywood he knew and loved.

Then came Disney. First the Paramount Theater was turned into the El Capitan, an ornate, rococo flagship for the Mouse's empire. Then came Hollywood and Highland, a monstrous, maze-like complex of stores, theaters, and giant, *Blade Runner*–like video screens, with a huge white elephant standing guard on top, as if to comment on the futility of it all. The centerpiece of the whole affair was the Kodak Theater, the permanent home of the Oscars. Only now it was the Dolby Theatre. So much for permanence.

Like Times Square in New York, only on a smaller scale, Hollywood was slowly being turned into a glitzy, family-friendly theme park, and Crush hated the transformation. Old banks and office buildings were being turned into high-priced condominiums and sushi restaurants and gaudy nightclubs. It was getting so he couldn't spot a wino or a hooker within a five-block radius. It just didn't feel like home.

To make matters so much more inconvenient, today was actually the day of the Oscar ceremony, which meant Hollywood Boulevard was blocked off to cars from La Brea to just before Vine Street. Crush had to park up on Franklin and walk two blocks down Cahuenga. It was February and it should have been cold and rainy, but, this being Los Angeles, it was eighty degrees and the sun was baking the concrete like the inside of an oven, a sensation that was emphasized by the scent of churros and tacos from the surrounding Mexican-food joints. Nothing could be further from the wet, romantic streets of the French Quarter. Crush felt his spirits lifting. They could take the look out of Hollywood, but the smells remained the same.

He checked to make sure the Letters of Transit were stored safely in his jacket pocket as he reached Hollywood and Vine. Looking down the street toward the Dolby Theatre, Crush was impressed by the security and police presence. They had this place locked down more than they would if the president were visiting.

Crush pondered whether this was because the Academy Awards offered such a tempting target for terrorists or because people in show business wanted to show how vital they were to American society. "Look how many guards we have!" the site seemed to cry out. "Aren't we valuable? Love us!"

◉

On the outside, 1500 Vine Street was an old art deco building that looked as if Philip Marlowe could have taken up business there and shared secretaries with Sam Spade and Jake Gittes. Inside, however, it looked new and space-age and awfully twenty-first century. Marlowe would not have been pleased.

Crush walked up to a uniformed security guard behind a console that would have looked at home on the starship *Enterprise*. "I'm here to see Sterling Bolsinger," he said, suddenly aware of his scruffy, unshaven appearance.

The guard looked him up and down. He didn't like what he saw. "And who shall I say is calling?" Crush told him and the security guard buzzed a connection on his headset. Once he got an answer that satisfied him, the guard directed Crush to a bank of elevators with no buttons. The guard controlled the elevators. Nothing was left to chance or the individual will of visitors in 1500 Vine.

Crush entered the elevator and when the doors shut, Crush was disturbed to note that there were no buttons on the inside of the elevator either. He was being sent to the tenth floor and the tenth floor only. There was no getting off early.

The elevator doors opened and Crush walked down a hallway painted in vivid, primary colors to apartment

1012. He raised his fist but a voice came from within before he could knock. "It's open. Come on in."

Crush stepped inside. The apartment was spacious
and decorated in an expensive, tasteful style. Crush hadn't
expected Sterling to be living this well. He couldn't
help but notice that among the mocha-colored sofas and
chairs, the well-stocked bookshelves, and the ancient Roman statuettes there was no movie memorabilia at all.
No posters from his many legendary movies, no signed
photographs of him standing with Kirk Douglas or Burt
Lancaster. Crush liked Sterling for that.

He was preparing coffee in the gleaming, stain-
less-steel kitchenette in front of a window that had a perfect view of the Hollywood sign. "Like the view?" Sterling
asked. "It's the view everybody on the East Coast imag-
ines everybody in Los Angeles has, am I right? Coffee?"

"Sure. I need to talk to Polly."

"She doesn't want to talk."

"To me?"

"To anybody."

"I need to talk to Rachel."

"Oh, she doesn't want to talk to you."

"They're in danger."

"Sorry, friend. I only have their cell phone numbers.
And they're ghosting me."

So Sterling knew the term, too. Crush felt out of the
loop. Then Sterling turned to Crush and he saw that the
right side of Sterling's face looked like it had been bashed
in and run along the sidewalk. His eye was swollen almost shut and his cheek had a butterfly bandage on a cut
that went almost from his lip to his ear. "What happened
to you?" Crush asked.

"This morning a bunch of goons jumped out of a

black sedan on Vine Street and grabbed me. They beat me up with real professional skill. I had to admire it. I think they were going to kill me until I convinced them that Adam had fired me. Then they made a call to somebody, apologized, and drove off."

"Who did they call?"

"I don't know. I can guess."

"Why did they let you go?"

"Because I'm not in Adam's orbit anymore. Don't you get it? Somebody wants to destroy Adam by taking away everything he loves. The only problem with that plan is Adam doesn't love anything but himself. Oh, well, I guess whoever's doing this is not a sociopath, so he just doesn't understand Adam Udell."

"Who? Who's behind all this?"

Sterling shrugged. "Meier Lustig. Isn't it obvious?"

"But why? Why would he go to all this trouble?"

"It's not that much trouble for a gang leader, is it? Killing Rachel's father, poisoning Byron, getting you arrested for murder, having me mugged in New Orleans? All in a day's work, I should think."

"But why? Just because Adam fucked his mistress?"

He put the coffee cup down and looked thoughtful. "As it turns out, it's a bit more complicated than that. I found out that Kristin Quinn wasn't Meier Lustig's mistress. She was his daughter."

Crush sat down. "How do you know that?"

"Well, the first clue was when the guy who was punching me in the face said, 'This is for Kristin. This is for Meier's daughter.' Then when I crawled back to the hotel, I looked Kristin up on Google. Turns out her real name is Christina Manheim. She's Meier's illegitimate daughter. But he looks after her. Supports her."

"So wait a minute. I don't understand. He killed his daughter because she was fucking Adam?"

"I don't think Meier killed his daughter."

"So she's alive?"

"I didn't say that." Sterling looked out the window. "We have to talk to someone who really knows what happened. Dr. ten Berge."

"I don't have time for that."

"You'll make time. She just got back from New Orleans. Rachel is staying with her."

◎

Sterling drove them to Malibu in his Tesla. Crush preferred old muscle cars, but he had to admire this ride. "Nice. You seem to be pretty well off. That apartment. This car."

"I made a good investment in my youth. A little company called IBM. You should check it out." He piloted the futuristic car to the 101 and drove west.

"I thought Rachel was with Adam."

"They broke up."

"That was fast."

"I thought so. They had some argument about his collection of movie memorabilia. She wanted him to get rid of it."

"Did he?"

"Apparently. But once he did, she left him."

"After three days?"

"Time passes quickly in La-La-Land."

"Why did she go to stay with ten Berge?"

Sterling shrugged. "You'll have to ask her."

"What exactly does Dr. ten Berge know about Adam

and Meier's daughter?"

"Dr. ten Berge knows everything about everybody," Sterling said. "She's the one you call when you're in trouble. I was drinking with her one night not too long ago. She got a little...loose lipped, shall we say. Started talking about things she shouldn't."

"Such as?"

"Better to have her tell it."

"What if she doesn't want to?"

"You're a big guy. You can persuade her, can't you?"

"I don't do torture. Tell me what you know."

"She said one night she got a call. She didn't say from who, but she said it was someone we both knew. Someone who was in the habit of slipping knockout juice to young ladies and having his way with them."

"Adam Udell."

"She wouldn't say for sure."

"You wouldn't think Adam would have to drug them to fuck them."

"She said he didn't have to, but he preferred it that way. That way he didn't have to listen to them talk."

Crush felt his jaw tighten and his stomach contract. He hated rape more than anything. He'd had too much first-hand knowledge of its horror and its consequences.

"I can see by your expression that you don't approve of Adam's little games," Sterling said.

"Do you?"

"What do you think? Anyway, this night something went wrong. The girl in question wasn't waking up. Could the good doctor come over and help? She went. There was your man and a couple of other men and this naked girl. They'd been doing her awhile before they sensed that something was wrong.

"Well, old Alva examined this girl and told them she was dead. What's more, she'd been dead for a couple of hours. So they'd been taking turns fucking a dead girl. Doc ten Berge thought that was hilarious."

"What did they do with her?"

Sterling shrugged. "She said they took her out and buried her somewhere."

"And you think it was Christina?"

"Well, at the time, I thought it was a sick joke. A tall tale. But now I'm not so sure. What if Adam did kill her? Even if he didn't mean to."

"If he just wanted to rape her?"

"I guess. What would he do then?"

"Did Adam know Christina was Lustig's daughter?"

"I don't think so. Lustig just seemed fond of her. Adam could only interpret that one way—that she was his lover. Adam might have thought he could sweep Lustig's mistress under the rug. But his daughter? No chance."

They glided into the driveway of a split-level house with an ocean view. Dr. ten Berge must have pulled in pretty good money for being there when she was needed.

"Do they know we're coming?" Crush asked.

"I thought it better if they didn't."

Sterling pressed the doorbell and got no answer. He tried the door and found it unlocked. They exchanged a look and walked in.

"Hello, Alva?" Sterling called out with somewhat forced cheer as he stepped into the living room. "Sterling here! Are you decent? I'm not, but only psychologically."

It was a stark, clean, orderly house, in keeping with Dr. ten Berge's personality. A row of Hummel figurines along the top row of the bookshelf provided a calculated hint of humanity.

Crush called out, "Rachel!" He didn't force a joke as he peeled off to the kitchen. He was too uneasy for that. There were three half-full cups of coffee sitting on the table. Crush dipped his finger in one and found it cold.

"Crush," Sterling called from down the hall, his voice sounding odd and strained. Crush hurried to find him in the master bedroom. He stood by the bed, looking a little lost and helpless. Dr. ten Berge was stretched out on the bed, elegantly dressed in a vintage black Valentino, eyes wide open, staring blankly at the ceiling. There were two red blossoms of gunshot wounds in her chest. Above her, written on the wall in bloody block letters, were the words: FOR CHRISTINA.

CHAPTER EIGHTEEN

Crush turned on his heels and went searching through the rest of the house. He found no sign of Rachel. So either she'd gotten away or somebody had taken her. He went back to the bedroom to find Sterling still staring at the body.

"I haven't seen anybody shot to death since I was in Korea," Sterling said in a whisper. "It hasn't gotten any better."

Crush felt ten Berge's wrist for a pulse, but it was just a formality. She looked like she'd been dead for hours. He looked up at the bloody writing on the wall. FOR CHRISTINA.

"FC," he said.

"What?" asked Sterling.

Crush didn't answer. He stared at the letters on the wall. They were bright red. Redder than any blood would be. He touched them and they felt slick and hard under his fingertips. He looked down at the nightstand next to the bed. Behind the clock and next to the iPhone there were two overturned bottles of red nail polish. He picked one of them up. It was empty.

"It's not written in blood?" Sterling asked.

"No. That's just set dressing."

"Maybe he wanted to write it in blood, but he didn't have the nerve."

"The nerve?"

"Well, come on, he'd have to stick his finger in the bullet hole and get it all bloody. Think about it. It would be disgusting."

Crush didn't want to think about it. He looked away, and that's when he noticed an iPad sitting on the chair across the room. It was propped up in its case, its screen facing the room, with a yellow Post-it note stuck to it. He walked over and looked down at the sticky note. It read: ADAM, PRESS PLAY.

He considered. Was Adam supposed to be here? Crush knew he shouldn't touch it himself. He should call the police and let them handle it.

He pressed play, but at least he used the hem of his T-shirt as a shield so he wouldn't leave a fingerprint. The screen flickered and a quick series of images appeared: hands bound, eyes staring, a woman's face looking out in fear. Was it Rachel? The face was gone before Crush could be sure.

It was replaced on the screen by another face, that of a handsome, dark-haired man of about sixty in a gray suit, shirt open at the top, with a thatch of gray chest hair showing, looking like a movie-of-the-week Israeli businessman. When he spoke it was with just a trace of a Middle Eastern dialect. "Hello, Adam," he said. "I hope you're well."

"It's him," Sterling said. "It's Meier Lustig. Why does he think Adam's here?"

"I am sorry about Alva," the man on the iPad continued. "But she was not exactly what they call an innocent bystander, was she? She was, at best, an accomplice after the fact. And I needed her to catch your attention. I knew you'd come to see her when I told you she was planning to talk to me." The man was beautifully lit, half in light, half in shadow, like in the opening of *The Godfather*. There was a long Italian word for it that Crush couldn't remember. Zerbe would know.

"The problem is this, Adam," he went on. "Dr. ten Berge *already* talked to me. She told me everything. So I know what you did to my beautiful daughter. That's why I know you aren't going to call the police. You don't want anyone to know that you are a murderer yourself."

He took a sip of water from a crystal tumbler and continued. "Now that I have your attention, what is it that I want to tell you? Only this. I have killed, or will kill, all those present at Christina's demise. Dr. Alva ten Berge. Lloyd Fury, that loathsome little man. Sterling Bolsinger—I expected better from him. Byron Douglas, your precious, idiotic movie star. I poisoned him once before and he would have died if not for that meddling bodyguard." He chuckled. "You see what I did there? That's a *Scooby-Doo* reference. Christina loved *Scooby-Doo*. She wanted to play Daphne in the reboot. She'll never get the chance now. You saw to that.

"But don't worry that I'm going to kill you, Adam. I'm not. You see, I'm dying myself, and I know death will only bring escape. Relief. Blessed oblivion. I don't want you to escape. I don't want you to forget. I want you to live with the memory of what you've done and what you've lost. The way I have. I want to take from you the things you love most. The way you took Christina from me.

"But the problem I'm faced with is this: what is it that you love most, Adam? You're such a delightfully, utterly selfish man. It's quite charming in small doses. Less so when it takes your little girl away from you forever.

"So what do you love most? I've already taken your

precious movie props. Rachel saw to that. Now we move on to the real thing. *Who* do you love the most? Is it Polly, who's stood by you for all those years and all those struggles? Or is it the new one, Rachel? Think about that while you're at the Oscars tonight. On your most special night of nights. Call me afterward, at midnight, and tell me. Think of it as your very own *Sophie's Choice*. Polly or Rachel. Decide.

"And think about this, too: I'll know if you choose the one you don't love, thinking I'll spare the other one. Then I'll just kill them both. And if I don't hear from you, if you try to evade the issue, then I'll also kill them both. The choice is yours.

"Oh, by the way, this message will self-destruct after you watch it once. I got that from *Mission: Impossible*. I do love movies, but you know that. And have a good time at the Oscars tonight. Break a leg!"

The screen went blank. The two men stared at the iPad.

"I wasn't there!" Sterling protested. "He's wrong about that. I wasn't there when Christina died. I have to talk to him. I have to explain."

"I don't think he's the explaining-to kind," Crush said. He tried to play the video again, but just got the spinning rainbow wheel of doom. The message had indeed self-destructed.

"Why did he think Adam would be here?" Sterling asked.

"I don't know. He must have sent Adam a message that either he didn't get or didn't care enough to act on."

"Does Meier have Rachel?"

"She's not here," Crush said.

"What about Polly?"

"Meier says he'll kill them both if he doesn't hear from Adam by midnight. He must have them."

"What can we do?" Sterling said. "We can't get hold of Adam. He's ghosting us. We don't know where he is."

Crush thought for a moment and grabbed some car keys off the bureau. "It's two-thirty. The Oscar ceremony starts at five. He wouldn't miss that for the world."

"So what?" Sterling said. "You can't get to him in there. You don't even have a ticket."

"I'm going to get one," Rush said. "Where does Byron Douglas live?"

◉

Byron Douglas lived in a modest mansion in Hancock Park, just a few blocks from Paramount Studios, where his sitcom *Family Practice* had been filmed (before a live studio audience) for the past eight years. He moved there in Year Two of the show, thinking he could walk or ride a bicycle to work. He did those things exactly one time each. The rest of the years he drove his various cars (a Hummer, a Mustang, an Aston Martin) through the ornate studio gates to his parking space right next to the sound stage. Convenience won over health and environmental concerns.

That was always the way with things, thought Byron as he fastened a cummerbund around his trim yet muscular waist. Whenever he tried to do the right thing, convenience came in and ruined it. Take today. The right thing to do was to take his daughter to the Oscars. She'd love it. She was sixteen and wildly impressed with the movie world—more than she'd ever been with her dad's boring old TV world. So it would have been a way to bridge the gap that had formed between the two of them since he'd split from her mother. He could hear them talking in the limo now, her eyes wide with wonder as they pulled up to walk the red carpet.

But it was difficult. For one thing, he'd have to call and talk to his ex-wife. She'd be cold and hostile, just as she'd been ever since he'd asked her to move to their Malibu house, for convenience's sake. And he'd have to wait until the disapproving and argumentative look faded from his daughter's eyes. He'd have to wonder whether she would ever look at him again the way she used to, when he was her daddy and could do no wrong.

It would just be easier to take Frida, even though Frida was just a passing fancy and would never be more than a glorious one-month stand. He could just roll over in bed and ask her to be his date to the Academy Awards. She'd kiss him and mount him and show her appreciation in various highly convenient ways.

So that's what Byron did. The road to hell, he reflected, had very little traffic, lots of rest stops, and was most convenient.

The doorbell rang. The doorbell seldom rang at Byron's house, and when it did it was usually UPS or FedEx delivery people or Seventh-day Adventists plying their trade. It couldn't be a friend or a business acquaintance. No one he knew ever dropped by without calling or texting first. So he let it go. But it rang again. Repeatedly. Insistently. And there was no one in the house to answer it but himself or Frida, and she was primping in the bathroom. This was one time convenience wouldn't save him.

Trudging to the door in his bare feet, his suspenders trailing behind him, he felt like an old man in an older movie. He had a few choice words for the rude man leaning on the doorbell outside. But when he flung the door open and saw that the man was that big bodyguard named Crush, he thought better of it. Crush was a huge, mean-looking man. And, besides, he'd saved his life. So he put on a big smile and said, "Cable Rush! How the hell are you?"

"It's Caleb," Crush said, "and I'm in a hurry."

"I'd love to help you with whatever, but I'm getting ready to go out. The Oscars, remember?"

"That's why I'm here." Crush walked by him and into the house. "You said you were presenting."

"Yeah, Documentary Short Subject. I even have some funny banter."

"Fine. I need to be your plus one."

Byron was a little taken aback by Crush's rude entrance, but he kept the smile on his face. "Sorry, I'm afraid that's taken. I'm going with Frida Ostroushko." *She really should have changed her name*, Byron reflected.

"Dump her," Crush said, standing in the middle of the foyer. "Take me instead."

Byron was flabbergasted. "Why?"

"Because I saved your life. You owe me a favor."

"I never said that."

"You didn't have to. It's understood."

"I'm going to have to ask you to leave?" That shouldn't have been a question, but Byron felt his inflection going up at the end of the sentence when he realized that, despite his weight training and muscle buildup, he'd clearly be no match in a fight with this man.

"Can Frida hear us?" Crush asked.

"Are you going to tell me what this is about?"

"You don't want me to talk about it if anyone can

hear."

Byron paused. There were many things he didn't want to talk about if anyone could hear. He led Crush into a library full of first editions that he'd never read and shut the door.

Crush told Byron he knew about Christina Manheim/ Kristin Quinn and her death. He told Byron he knew he was at the scene. Then he told Byron that Christina was Meier Lustig's daughter.

Byron sat down, poured himself a straight Scotch, downed it, and coughed for five minutes. He wiped his eyes.

"I didn't know she was Lustig's daughter," Byron said. "Not that it matters. It was a terrible thing to do anyway. I didn't know that Adam had drugged her. Not at first. I thought she was willing."

"But passed out?"

"I thought she was drunk! Passed-out drunk."

"But willing? So you took turns fucking her?"

"When you say it that way, it sounds bad. But a lot of people get drunk before they fuck. Loosens them up, you know. It wasn't like she was fighting us off."

"She was dead."

"That I didn't know! I would never have touched her if I'd known that."

"It's nice that you have some standards."

"So what is this? Are you blackmailing me?"

"Blackmailing you into giving me your plus one? No." He told Byron the rest. How Polly Coburn's and Rachel Strayhorn's lives were at stake unless he could get to Adam before midnight.

"But Rachel's supposed to be at the Oscars tonight," Byron said.

"I don't think she's going to make it."

Byron's first thought was that if Rachel Strayhorn were to die, it would totally kill the already damaged chances of *The Rage Machine II: Redemption* ever seeing the light of day. His second thought was that he was a total asshole for thinking that. He must redeem himself, in real life if not on the screen. "Did Meier really say he tried to kill me?"

"He did," Crush said.

"So it wasn't God reaching out to me after all?"

"He works in mysterious ways."

"I didn't really think it was God. I was just hoping."

"Sorry to disappoint you."

"I mean, why would God speak to me?"

"Why would He speak to anybody?"

"And Meier said he was going to kill me?"

"He said that."

"Do you think he meant it?"

"He killed Lloyd and Dr. ten Berge. I think he means it."

"Will you protect me?"

"Sure. But first I have to get to Adam."

"All right," Byron said. "Let's go. The limo is waiting out front."

"Don't you have to explain it to Frida?"

Byron hesitated. "It would be more convenient not to."

◎

The driver went down Melrose to Highland, piloting the long, sleek limo the five miles from Larchmont to Hollywood. It should have taken them ten minutes. They gave themselves an hour. Oscar traffic was a nightmare.

In the spacious back seat of the limo, Crush changed into the spare tuxedo Byron had gotten just in case his

Armani didn't pass muster. The Ralph Lauren had a straight necktie, not a bow tie, so Byron had rejected it. What was the point of wearing a tuxedo if it just looked like a business suit? So Crush slipped on the Ralph Lauren abomination. Once Crush had all the parts in the right places, he looked pretty good in it, Byron had to admit. They made an attractive, manly couple.

"Do you think people will think I'm coming out?" Byron asked.

"What do you mean?"

"If I walk down the red carpet with you. Do you think people will think I'm gay?"

"I don't care."

"I mean, don't get me wrong. You're a good-looking guy, and I don't think there's anything wrong with being gay."

"I really don't care."

"It's just that there were a lot of rumors about my sexual preferences a couple years ago."

"I don't know how to make it more clear for you..."

"It was on account of Donny, my co-star on the show."

"I don't care at all."

"Donny's gay. And we used to hang out a lot. But just 'cause you hang out with a gay guy doesn't make you gay. Okay, I had sex with him a couple of times, just to see what it was like. But that doesn't mean I identify as gay."

"Can you stop talking?"

They were in line for the drop-off at the Dolby Theatre. It was still broad daylight, but all the stars were getting out of their limos in formal evening wear, since the broadcast was scheduled for prime time on the East Coast. Movie people are used to day-for-night.

They pulled up to the security tent, got out, presented

their tickets, went through the metal detectors, and came out the other side to the red carpet. The cameras flashed. The crowd of onlookers gave an appreciative gasp when it spotted Byron. Not the sizable roar it gave to George Clooney and Leo DiCaprio, but enough to make Byron feel the love. Next, he was directed toward the Step and Repeat—that long backdrop where the photographers and reporters can capture celebrities at their most calculatedly casual.

◉

While Byron was distracted by TV interviewers, Crush went up the huge flight of red-carpeted stairs to the theater itself. The broadcast was starting in forty-five minutes. Now was the time for the elite to mill about in the lobby and anoint one other with their presences. Crush stationed himself against a wall in the lobby and scanned the crowd. It occurred to him that he was acting like the bouncer he normally was. Keeping an eye out for trouble; trying to spot a suspicious person among the multitude.

Famous faces and bodies abounded. The gowns and the jewelry assaulted Crush's eyes. Zerbe would have loved to be here, but to Crush the stars were merely an annoyance, people who stood between him and his goal. His was the only face that registered disappointment when Johnny Depp or Matthew McConaughey walked past. Where was Adam? Had he missed him? Had he gone into the theater and taken his seat? Or had he decided not to come after all? Had fear won out over the lust for glory?

Crush almost missed spotting Adam going into the bathroom. He wasn't wearing his trademark black jacket and T-shirt. Instead he was in an all-black tux with a black dress shirt. Crush spotted him just as he darted into the men's room, his black cowboy boots disappearing behind the closing door.

◎

In the elegant bathroom, Adam stepped up to a urinal and sighed as he unzipped his pants. He had so much on his mind that he almost couldn't pee. And now there was this big guy moving in next to him. Didn't this asshole know that standard pissing etiquette states that you don't stand next to somebody unless all the other urinals are taken? Or was he coming on to Adam? He cast a furtive eye over toward his intrusive neighbor's equipment and was startled by what he saw. It was not that the dick was particularly big or particularly small. It was that it was not out at all. The guy was just standing next to Adam and not peeing. The nerve of some people.

"Adam, it's me," the big man said. "Don't look startled."

Adam looked up. "Crush," he said, his expression turning ashen.

"That, don't do that," Crush said.

"I'm sorry."

"For what?"

"For framing you. I didn't know what else to do."

"Never mind about that. Now we're going to turn around and we're going to walk out of here."

"I can't leave."

"Yes, you can."

"But I'm nominated. What if I win?"

"You'll still have won. And Rachel and Polly will be

alive."

"Lustig has them?"

"Yes."

"I wondered why Rachel wasn't here. What are we going to do?"

"We're going to talk to Lustig."

"I'm afraid."

"Don't be afraid of him. Be afraid of me. Do you know what I could do to you, right here and now?"

"You'll never get away."

"I wouldn't want to."

The two men stood at their respective urinals, looking at each other.

"Is she really in danger?" Adam asked.

"Who? Who are you worried about? Polly or Rachel?"

Adam didn't answer. He just said, "Let's go."

CHAPTER NINETEEN

Leaving the Oscars ceremony was like being a salmon swimming upstream. The whole flow of nature was going into the theater while they were going out. Adam called for his limo driver, and they had to wait an interminable amount of time for him to arrive.

Once he did, Crush opened the driver's door and told him to get out. The driver looked stunned and refused. Adam told him to do it and gave him fifty dollars to pay for a cab to take him home.

Crush slid behind the wheel and Adam got in the passenger seat. Crush waited for the traffic to open up and then sped away. "Where does Meier live?" he asked.

"Holmby Hills," Adam said. "Next to the Playboy Mansion. Do you know where that is?"

Crush knew. He turned down Highland, cursing every stoplight. He told Adam everything about Dr. ten Berge's death and the video Meier had left for him.

"I don't understand. What do I do when I get to Meier's house?" Adam asked.

"You say you're sorry."

"And then what?"

"It's up to him."

"Will he let Polly and Rachel go?"

"If you're offered in exchange."

"Is that what I'm going to do?"

"That's what *I'm* going to do."

Adam was silent for a few blocks. "I'm sorry about what happened in the cemetery."

"I don't care about that now."

"I panicked. The guy was attacking Rachel."

"What guy?"

"Brandon Renbourn. I pulled out my gun. I told him to stop. Then this other man jumped out. I shot him. I was aiming at his arm but I hit him right in the head. I killed him. He died." Adam was starting to cry. Crush couldn't believe it. "A human being died and I killed him."

"You've killed before."

"That was different! With Kristin it was an accident. I'd given lots of girls Propofol before. Then I play-rape them. It's just play. It's entirely consensual."

"That's what Bill Cosby said." Crush had to fight the impulse to throw Adam from the speeding car, to watch him crushed by oncoming traffic. But not now. He needed Adam alive.

"It's true!" said Adam. "I don't know what went wrong that time. She was willing, I swear. She must have had an allergic reaction. It wasn't my fault."

"Did you know she was Lustig's daughter?"

"No! I didn't know that till just now, when you told me. I'd never have played with her if I'd known that. I thought she was his mistress."

"Tell him that. I'm sure it'll make it all better."

"When I shot the guy in the cemetery, I went over and looked at him. I recognized him as one of Meier's men. I thought I was really fucked then."

"Whose idea was it to give me the gun?"

"I think it was mutual. Rachel said we could make it look like you shot him. She said you were smart, you'd be able to find a way out of it."

"It's nice of her to have so much faith in me."

"But we couldn't leave the body out there for you to deal with. That would be too cruel. So we loaded it into the crypt and put it in the casket. I thought it would be safe there. Who would look in there?"

"But if somebody did, I'd take the blame?"

"I said I was sorry," said Adam.

"Tell the New Orleans police that."

"Oh, God..." Adam lapsed into a sulk. Crush turned left at Carolwood. "After that I was a changed man, Crush. I couldn't go on making movies with shootings and killings in them. Not after I saw a man die that way. I shut down *The Rage Machine*. I asked Rachel to marry me."

"So a happy ending all around."

"We got married in Vegas. That night, Rachel told me the truth about herself. How she was being blackmailed by Lustig so he could get his hands on my collection. I didn't care. I loved her. I thought she loved me. I gave her my junk so she could give it to him. I loved her that much. Then she disappeared. I thought she left me after she got what she wanted. I thought she was just playing me. Meier called me a couple of times, left me messages. I didn't listen to them. I thought he was just taunting me, just rubbing my nose in it."

"He was telling you that Dr. ten Berge was going to tell him about what happened to Christina. He was trying to lure you to her house. So you'd watch the video."

"That means Rachel didn't leave me. That means she was kidnapped."

"She *did* leave you. She went to Dr. ten Berge's house."

"But that's not really leaving, is it? That's more like a separation. That's more like her thinking about it, exploring her options. That's not *leaving* leaving."

"You can talk yourself into believing anything, can't you?"

"Doesn't everybody do that? How else do we cope with this fucked-up world?"

Crush pulled up to the iron gates of Meier Lustig's mansion. A brick column with a camera at eye level greeted him as he rolled down his window and reached out to press the call button. A gruff voice came out of the speaker. "Yes?"

"We're here." Crush leaned to the side so the camera could see Adam.

"Who's here?" said the voice.

"Tell Lustig I have Adam Udell."

There was the sound of movement from the speaker. Voices chattering in the distance. Then another voice came over the speaker. "Adam! What are you doing here? Why aren't you at the Oscars? It's your big night." The voice was gentler than the other one, with a more musical lilt to it.

"I want to talk to you," Adam said.

"Go back to the Oscars," the voice said with a laugh.

Crush reached into his pocket and pulled the Letters of Transit out. He held them up to the camera. "You see what this is?"

Silence from the speaker. Then, "All right, come in." The gates slowly swung open.

◉

The house looked like Wayne Manor from the old *Batman* TV series. But then most of the houses in Holmby Hills looked like Bruce Wayne's place in one way or another.

Sure, some had a more *Wuthering Heights*, Tower of London, or Moorish vibe, but they all looked like they'd been transplanted from some other country and some other time. The modern age just wasn't cool enough for the rich folks who lived on the hill.

As Crush and Adam ran up the stone steps to the massive front door, it was opened by a goon who mumbled, "Gimme the letters."

"I'll give them to Lustig myself," Crush said.

The guy shrugged and turned and led them through a Tudor great hall to a huge set of double doors. He opened them, and Crush and Adam followed him into the living room of any suburban house, circa 1985. The room was decorated in a humble, homey style totally at odds with the grandiosity of the house itself. Sofas. Easy chairs. A coffee table. A credenza over to the side stocked with dip and chips and cold beers. A group of people who looked like wholesome relatives at a family Thanksgiving populated the room.

On the big TV screen, the Oscars ceremony was in progress. All the guests listened with rapt attention to Jimmy Fallon as he made the standard putting-down-the-stars-but-loving-them-too jokes. The goon stepped up to a La-Z-Boy recliner and leaned in to speak to its occupant. "He wants to give you the letters himself."

The man in the recliner sighed. He closed up the La-Z-Boy with a grunt and stood, turning to Crush and Adam. He was a middle-aged man with a dark complexion who looked like he might have been Meier Lustig's less formal, more approachable brother. "Come into the den, Adam. And bring your friend."

They followed him through a door near the credenza into a room filled with Adam Udell's treasures. The ray guns, the sled, the black bird—all of it cluttering up the room, like at the end of *Citizen Kane* and *Raiders of the Lost Ark*. It was a clearinghouse for the stuff that Hollywood dreams were made of.

Closing the door behind them, the man turned to Adam. "So you have the Letters of Transit?"

Adam gestured to Crush. "He does."

"I appreciate you completing the collection," he said, gesturing to the memorabilia, "but you really didn't have to do it tonight."

"I want to see Meier Lustig," Crush said.

The man glanced at Adam. "He's a joker?"

"Hand them over, Crush," Adam said. "This *is* Meier."

Crush hesitated. "You're Meier Lustig?"

"That's what my mother tells me."

"Did you make a video for Adam?"

"Have you had a head injury, Bub? I notice the bandage."

"You didn't kill Dr. ten Berge?"

The man turned to Adam. "What the hell's he talking about?"

"Or Lloyd Fury?"

"What the fuck? Is this a gag?"

"Was Christina Manheim your daughter?" Crush asked.

"Who?"

"Kristin Quinn, then."

"Oh, Kristin! She was a sweet girl. I really should be angry at Adam here for taking her from me. But there's more where she came from. All this," he spread his hands to take in the treasure trove, "is one of a kind."

"So she's not your daughter."

"Of course not. Quit saying that, it's unseemly. She was nothing more than a fine piece of ass. Special, but thoroughly replaceable."

Crush handed over the letters. The man took them to a table and examined them closely. He looked up at Adam. "They're good. Good copies. Not originals. Now why are you here? Get back to the Oscars. You should still have time to be there when you lose the director's award."

Crush stared at the man who said he was Meier Lustig. The man on the video had looked enough like him to have been cast as him in a movie, and Crush could understand how he'd been fooled. But there was one person who hadn't been fooled. The realization tumbled into place. He grabbed Adam by the arm. "We have to go."

"Go where?"

Crush didn't answer, he just hustled Adam out into the living room.

"Best of luck tonight," Meier called after him. "You know Ridley Scott is going to win Best Director, but I'm rooting for you!"

◉

As Crush drove the limo out through the gates, Adam was demanding an explanation. "What made you think Lustig was behind all this?"

"The video."

"Who was in the video?"

"It doesn't matter. Some actor."

"What do you mean? It was like a scene? From a movie?"

"Exactly like a movie. I should have known that video was too well made."

"But why did you think the guy in the video was

Lustig?"

"Because Sterling Bolsinger said it was."

"That's crazy. Sterling knows Meier. He wouldn't..." Adam fell silent for a moment. "Fuck. That old fuck. Why would he do this? I've done nothing but help that man. People had forgotten all about him before I rediscovered him. He should be grateful!"

"He killed Dr. ten Berge. He killed Lloyd Fury. He must have his reasons. He said he has a house on Mulholland Drive. You know where it is?"

"Sure. But is he there? With Polly and Rachel? Wouldn't he be hiding?"

"No. He wants me to bring you to him. That's why he did this. So I'd track you down and bring you to him."

"Shouldn't we call the police?"

Crush glanced over at Adam. "Sure. What's the address? So I can tell them where to go."

Adam told him the address, and he entered it into the limo's GPS. He kept driving.

"Aren't you going to call?" Adam asked.

"No. If he hears the police coming he'll kill them. He wants you."

"So what are you going to do?"

"Give you to him," Crush said.

Adam nodded solemnly. "So that's it."

"That's what?"

"That's your price. The safety of those you love. I told you I'd figure it out. Do I know people or what?"

"What's Sterling's price then?"

Adam was uncomfortably silent.

CHAPTER TWENTY

When Christina Manheim, Sterling Bolsinger's only child, was born in 1995, he was more annoyed than delighted. After all, he hadn't known Christina's mother all that well, and he was distracted by the slow death of his career. He hadn't directed a theatrical feature in five years. He'd only done two in the eight years before that, both low-budget horror pictures of the type he'd never even have considered during his heyday. The only viable project being offered him was a biopic of Woodrow Wilson for HBO. This was hardly on the level of the Steven McQueen and Paul Newman pictures he'd helmed in the sixties and seventies, but at least it didn't involve a mad scientist or a psycho killer. And Sterling had begun in television, after all, directing a *Playhouse 90* starring James Dean and written by Reginald Rose. This was going full circle, wasn't it?

With this on his mind, the last thing he needed was a paternity suit. Michelle Manheim was a receptionist at his agent's office, and Sterling had taken her out a few times, more out of boredom than out of desire. When she told him she was pregnant, he assumed it was a prelude to asking for money either to fund an abortion or to support the squalling child for the rest of its damned life.

But Michelle didn't ask for anything. She just told Sterling that she was pregnant and left it at that. He waited for the other shoe to drop. It didn't. *He* had to contact *her*. *Perhaps*, he thought, *this is her strategy. Maybe she wants me to chase her.* But, in truth, she didn't have a strategy. She was just having a baby, and she really didn't give a damn whether she heard from Sterling Bolsinger ever again.

So he started calling her once a week. Sending her checks, which she promptly tore up and sent back to him. On the phone, she was polite, keeping him informed as to her condition and her well-being. But there was little fondness in her voice and less caring. It was almost as if she had used him as a sperm donor, he thought. An Oscar-winning, A-list-director sperm donor. He felt used. Pissed off. At once grateful and deeply offended that she wasn't making any demands on him.

He was prepping for the *Wilson* production when he got the email that she was in labor. So he had to leave the first production meeting he'd had in five years to go see her. It was really annoying.

By the time he got to the hospital, Christina was already born. This annoyed him even more. If he was going to go through all the trouble of driving through rush hour traffic, he ought to at least be able to witness the birth.

Then Sterling saw Christina. In her mother's arms. So tiny and helpless and beautiful. He'd never known that something could be more valuable than even his own self. It was love at first sight.

Michelle didn't accept financial help, but she did allow Sterling to visit, once every two weeks. He could have gone to court and demanded more, he supposed, but he was pretty content to have things her way. He got the pleasures of fatherhood without any of the responsibilities. He got the joy of watching her grow up into a child, then a teenager, and then a woman. All the while, he grew into an old man. It was enough to break the strongest heart.

Christina went to USC and Michelle did let Sterling help with the tuition. At that time, Christina hadn't been told that he was her father. He was just the guy who came to visit, the honorary uncle, the friend of the family. There was nothing romantic between her mother and him. She had other boyfriends, and Christina watched them come and watched them go. But Sterling was a constant presence.

Then, in Christina's last year in college, her mother was in a car accident. A drunk driver sped through a red light and T-boned her Civic. It happens all the time, every day.

He didn't make it to the hospital in time for that, either. He found Christina crying in the hallway. Suddenly an orphan. He tried to comfort her, told her she wasn't alone. She didn't seem to want to listen, but he persisted. He chose what he realized afterward was the worst possible time to tell Christina he was her father.

Her reaction was not what he expected. She didn't find comfort or relief in the information. Instead she reacted coldly, like he'd slapped her. "You're not telling me anything I don't already know," she said. And she clammed up and didn't talk to him again. For two years.

In retrospect he decided she'd been lying, she hadn't known about his being her father. She was engaging in defensive behavior, and he could see why. Her mother had been taken from her, and now this old man was trying to take her place. If he'd written the scene, it would have played just like that.

He tried to contact her time and again. Finally, two

years later, he succeeded in setting a date with her for
coffee. He'd been following her "career" as an actress
and model, which had been going nowhere. He sat her
down and proceeded to tell her everything she was doing
wrong with her life. It was quite a list.

After half an hour he realized he had been doing all
the talking. He tried to draw her out, but she just nodded
and looked amused. In desperation, he offered her a job
as an intern with his production company, which was
currently keeping alive its seven-year streak of producing
exactly nothing. She accepted, paid for her coffee, and
left.

If he'd thought being her boss was going to improve
their relationship he was sadly mistaken. She was a good
worker, nothing more. She would not allow the freeze
between them to thaw.

Neither of them told anyone the truth about their relationship. If she remembered the kindly uncle she used
to play with when she was a child, she didn't show it.

She just did research for him, for films he knew he
would never make. One of them involved the Israeli mob
and its branches in LA. That was how she met Meier
Lustig, an old acquaintance of Sterling's. It was a relationship he wasn't proud of, and he got very uneasy when
Christina and Lustig started spending time together.
Could she sense his ambivalence toward the mobster?
Was that why she gravitated toward him? Or was Sterling
being egotistical, assuming that he was the cause of all of
her bad decisions?

Whatever the reason, Christina became Lustig's mistress. Sterling was tortured by the relationship, but he
couldn't tell Lustig to back off, that she was his daughter. It would be too humiliating. So he choked back his

emotions and closed his eyes.

But when Adam Udell offered Christina a part in his latest movie, Sterling saw a way out. A way for her to work more closely with her father. A way for her to start a career outside of the shadow of that gangster. And if Adam wanted to date her a little, well, what was the harm in that? The way to success for a woman, Sterling knew, was often through the bedsheets of powerful men. Adam's motley entourage of Lloyd Fury, Dr. ten Berge, Polly, and Rachel made for dubious chaperones.

But then Christina disappeared. Without a trace. Gone. She'd cut Sterling off from her life before, but this seemed more permanent, more scarily concrete. Had Lustig gotten jealous and taken violent action? Or had she merely run away?

It wasn't until two months ago, when he'd been sharing a drunken conversation with Alva ten Berge, that he'd learned the truth. The truth about what Adam and his friends had done to his beautiful girl.

The truth had changed him. The truth had given him a purpose. The truth had given him a last story to tell. One last production to throw himself into: *Revenge*.

At first he simply sent letters to Adam, supposedly from Meier Lustig, threatening him. Just to see what he'd do. Adam was frightened but not *too* frightened. Just mildly worried. He'd have to do more.

When he learned that Adam had no intention of helping him get his *Don Quixote* film off the ground, that instead he was going to appropriate it for himself, he decided he had to take action. Action that would achieve its climax tonight. The night of the Oscars.

The first thing to do was to poison Byron Douglas. This would kill two birds with one stone. Obviously it would kill Byron, who'd been one of those present when Christina died. But it would also kill Adam's big-budget picture deader than dead. What was *The Rage Machine* without its Enforcer? That would really hurt Adam where he lived.

It wasn't hard for Sterling to get his hands on the Propofol. He was one of Adam's inner circle, after all, and could come and go as he pleased. He substituted it for Byron's HGH and waited.

Unfortunately, Crush had thwarted that plan, so with Lloyd, Sterling decided to be more direct. He saw Lloyd with Rachel and followed him back to his cheap motel. The next morning he showed up and blew Lloyd's head off. Sterling hadn't shot anybody since Korea, but it came back pretty easily.

Things were looking up.

Then Adam fouled things up by being Adam and cutting Sterling out of his inner circle. If he didn't have easy access to Adam, how could this production continue?

He knew if anybody could find Adam and bring him to Sterling it would be Crush. Crush didn't worry about niceties or politics. If he wanted something he just went and got it. The trick was to give Crush the proper motivation, and he knew how to work with difficult actors.

So he hired a shyster lawyer and had him issue veiled threats about Rachel and Polly, people Crush cared about deeply. Then came the fun part.

Sterling hired an actor and produced a video. A video made for a very specific audience of one: Crush. It felt good to be back in the director's seat.

He just had to go to Dr. ten Berge's house, kill her, kidnap Rachel, and plant the video. When he got there, he found them getting dressed for the Oscars. Dr. ten

Berge was Rachel's plus one. Killing her was easy—he'd never liked Alva, and after that first killing, it came naturally. Kidnapping Rachel was surprisingly easy, too. The gun was awfully persuasive.

Sterling took her to his house on Mulholland and locked her in the basement. Then he set up his living room with his flatscreen TV, his five heavy Craftsman-style chairs in front of it, his coffee table, and his crudités. All for his Oscars party.

Polly showed up early, because he'd asked her to help and because she didn't have anywhere else to be that day. She even brought her Oscars ballot, all filled out. Getting her subdued, however, wasn't easy. She fought like a wild animal, but he finally got her bound, gagged, and strapped to one of the chairs.

Then Crush called and Sterling said he'd meet him at his new apartment. His newly beaten face, courtesy of Polly, made the story of his assault at the hands of Lustig's men that much more convincing.

Yes, the production was going off without a hitch. But now he was getting worried. The Oscar broadcast was progressing, and Polly and Rachel were tied to their chairs in front of the TV. Crush should already have arrived with Adam, the star of the production.

Wasn't it always like a star to be late?

CHAPTER TWENTY-ONE

Sterling's house on Mulholland was a low-slung, single-story ranch affair built in the middle of the last century. A mansion that looked like a simple suburban home, for the unpretentiously wealthy. A vanished breed.

Crush pulled up three houses away around a curve in the road and turned to Adam. "All right. You're going to knock on the door. You're going to go in."

"I don't think so," Adam whispered.

"I think you will. You want to help them. Polly and Rachel."

"I do," he said. "I want to help them. But I can't go up to that door. I just can't. What if he really killed Alva and Lloyd? I can't."

"Yes, you can," Crush said in his most soothing tone. "You want to make up for what you've done, don't you? For what you did to Kristin. For what you did to me. For what you did to Bub."

"Who's Bub?"

"See, you don't even know his name. The guy you shot in the cemetery. You have to make up for that."

"I could give Sterling money."

"Money won't fix this. He wants you. You have to man up."

"I hate that phrase."

"So do I. But it fits. Be a man. Go to that door."

"What are you doing to do?"

"I'll be right behind you. Once you distract him."

"Then you'll take him out?"

"I'll try."

"That's not very reassuring."

"It's all I've got," Crush said, opening the car door and getting out. Adam got out too, moving slowly but moving all the same.

The moon was full, and the low haze in the sky caught the city lights and reflected them back so that the street looked straight out of a day-for-night scene in an old MGM movie. They walked toward Sterling's house. Crush stopped at the curb, taking in the scene.

"What are you doing?" Adam whispered.

"I'm looking," Crush replied.

"Trying to figure out your strategy?"

"Just looking."

"How 'bout that window?" Adam pointed to a big plate-glass window next to the front door, hedged in by shrubs and tall trees. "You could dive through it while I distract Sterling at the front door."

"If I want to get lacerated by shattered glass. This isn't a movie. That's not a breakaway window."

"So what are you going to do?"

"I have an idea. Trust me." Crush walked toward the front door, confident that Adam would follow, which he did. In truth, he had no idea what he was going to do. But he had faith that something would come to him in the moment.

◎

The doorbell rang just as they were announcing the Best Supporting Actress. Rachel lost.

"Man, I really thought you were going to win it, Rachel," Sterling said, "but I guess Judi Dench has more fans."

"Fuck you, Sterling," Rachel said as she struggled against the zip ties that held her fast to the chair. Polly just glared at Sterling and bit at the cloth gag in her mouth, as if she wished she could feel his flesh in her teeth.

Sterling got up to answer the door. He was nervous enough that he almost forgot his gun. He had to circle back to the coffee table to pick up his Glock. He pulled back the slide, then opened the door a crack, making sure the chain was still in place. You couldn't be too careful these days.

Adam Udell stood on the front step.

"Adam," Sterling said, brightly. "You made it! Great! It really wasn't an Oscar party without you. Is Byron here, too?"

"No," Adam said, not sure what tone to take. "He couldn't make it."

"Well, shit. I wanted to have everybody together. Oh well, Crush is here, right?"

"Uh..." Adam hesitated.

Sterling showed Adam his gun through the gap in the door. That was what Crush had been waiting for. He pushed Adam aside and kicked at the door, putting his full two hundred and fifty pounds against the flimsy chain. The door flew open, knocking the gun out of Sterling's hand. Crush leapt through the doorway, his shoulder driving Sterling to the floor. The old man was in good shape but he was no match for Crush.

Adam peered in through the doorway, timidly. Crush

looked around for the gun. It had skittered across the floor to the foot of a high-backed Craftsman chair with sturdy wooden arms. Looking up, he saw Rachel in a lovely red dress, strapped into the chair with plastic ties around her wrists, arms, ankles, calves, and throat. She stared at Sterling with pure hate in her eyes. "Take that, motherfucker!" she said.

Polly was tied to an identical chair next to Rachel, her mouth stuffed with a rag that was duct-taped to her face. She was spitting and coughing what sounded like swear words of her own into the rag. Next to them were three empty chairs, all arranged in a row in front of the TV. On the TV, Elton John was singing his Oscar-nominated song from the latest Pixar epic, but no one in the room was paying attention.

"Kill the bastard, Crush," Rachel said.

Crush stood up. "You want me to kill him, Rach? Is that what you want me to do? Is it?"

His challenging tone seemed to surprise her. "What's the matter, Crush?"

"I told him, Rachel," Adam said. "I told him about what happened in the cemetery. How we framed him."

"You fucking idiot," Rachel said.

"Yeah, he's the fucking idiot," Crush said. "Everybody's the fucking idiot. Everybody but you."

Polly worked the rag out of her mouth. "Get the gun, Caleb."

Crush took a deep breath. He stepped over Sterling to pick up the gun. Just then, the big picture window shattered into a thousand pieces as a man's body flew through it and landed on the floor, doing a drop and roll like the hero from an action movie. It was Rachel's stalker, Brandon Renbourn. He tried to stand, but blood flowed from his fingers and his hands. He looked surprised as it spurted from his throat like water from a punctured garden hose.

Crush watched in stunned silence as Brandon dropped to his knees and whispered, "Rachel, I love you." He fell to the floor in a widening pool of blood.

Polly and Sterling gasped in horror. Adam gave a high-pitched scream. Rachel shook her head and whispered, "You stupid fucking idiot."

But Sterling reacted quickly, crawling across the floor to reach his gun. Crush saw what he was doing a second too late. Sterling grabbed the Glock and flipped over. Crush started for him. Sterling pointed the gun and fired.

Crush felt a burning pain in his gut. He reached down and felt a wound on the left side of his stomach.

"Don't come any closer," Sterling said. "I don't want to kill you. But I will."

"I think you already have," Crush said, falling to his knees.

Sterling stood up, wobbly but triumphant. "I didn't want to kill *him* either." He looked regretfully at Brandon as he bled out on the floor.

Crush tried to plug the bullet hole with his fingers.

Sterling crossed to the coffee table and threw him a cloth napkin. "Try to stop the bleeding. Sit down and watch." He gestured toward the empty chair. "You, too," he said to Adam. Sterling grabbed the remote and turned up the volume on the TV. "We don't want to miss the climax of the evening."

◎

Robert Downey Jr. and Chris Evans were doing lame

patter about superhero movies before they gave the award for Best Special Effects while Crush sat in the chair to the right of Polly, pressing the blood-soaked napkin into the bullet wound in his gut. The bleeding had slowed on the outside, anyway. Internally, there was no telling what was going on. He looked over at Rachel, in her striking scarlet gown, and started laughing.

"What's so funny?" Rachel asked.

"I was just wondering...who are you wearing?"

"Fuck you, Crush."

"How are you doing, Caleb?" Polly asked. Sterling hadn't put the duct tape back on her mouth.

"I'm dying...but slowly. It hurts like hell."

"We'll make it out of here," she said.

"That's nice of you to say. But I really doubt it."

"I refuse to give up," Polly said. She was struggling, trying to lift her right wrist, trying to pry the arm of the old wooden chair free. *She might make it happen*, Crush thought. *Give her a few days.*

Sterling paced in front of the TV. "Okay, after the next commercial break they're presenting Best Score, then Best Director. Are you ready, Adam?"

But Adam, sitting in the chair next to Rachel, wasn't paying attention. He kept staring at Brandon's limp body lying on the floor in a pool of blood. "Who the hell is that?" he asked. He'd been asking that for several minutes, and Crush was getting tired of hearing it.

"It's Rachel's stalker," Crush said, through a grimace of pain. "Brandon Renbourn."

"What was he doing here?"

"He was trying to rescue me, okay?" Rachel said.

"How did he know you were here?"

Rachel shrugged. "Lucky guess?"

"Shut up!" Sterling barked. "He doesn't matter. This is *my* show. I'm in charge here. Pay attention. They're presenting the award for Best Musical Score."

"Alexandre Desplat has that sewn up," Polly said.

"Are you wondering why I'm having you watch this, Adam?"

"I'm wondering why you're doing everything, Sterling. What did I ever do to you?"

Sterling stopped and stared at him. "You haven't figured that out yet? Well, I'll explain soon. But I want everything to be timed out perfectly. That's something you young punks just don't understand—timing. Every movie you make is two and a half hours long and has three different endings. You don't know how to pace things!"

"Is that why you're doing this? Because you don't like my movies?"

"That's one of the reasons. Let me tell you how it will go. They'll announce the Best Director. Who will it be, Polly?"

"Ridley Scott, no question."

"At that moment, when your dreams of glory are dashed, I will kill the one you love the most. Then I will kill myself. Boom. The end. And you will have to live with the consequences."

"Why don't you kill yourself first," Crush said, "to make sure you don't forget."

"I'm not talking to you!" Sterling said. "I'm talking to Adam."

"Why are you doing this?" Adam asked.

Sterling turned to Crush. "You know why. Tell him why."

"For Christina," Crush said.

"Christina? I don't know any Christina!" Adam said.

"Kristin Quinn, then. That girl you used and discarded."

"Oh, God. I'm sorry about that. It was an accident."

"She was my daughter!" Sterling said.

"What? Why the fuck didn't you tell me? I wouldn't have touched her!"

"Well, it didn't occur to me that you'd try to gang rape her. I thought you were just giving her a part in your fucking movie."

"But she was Meier's mistress."

"She just did that to spite me. Because she hated me. She was ashamed to be my daughter."

"If I'd known, Sterling, I swear..."

"Shut up! It doesn't matter whether you knew or not. From the moment Dr. ten Berge told me what you'd done, I plotted this. I planned this. I *directed* this. Just like I directed that video. Wasn't it perfect, Crush?"

"It was okay," Crush said.

"And everything I had that actor say was the truth. My truth."

"So you're dying?" Crush asked.

"I'm eighty-six years old. Of course I'm dying." Sterling pointed the gun at Polly's head. "Now, Adam, tell me. Which one do you love the most?"

Adam stared at Polly, wide-eyed. Sterling moved the gun to Rachel's head. "This one?" He pivoted, pointing the gun back at Polly, who shut her eyes and kept working on the arm of her chair. "Or this one?"

Adam blurted out, "I don't know. I don't even know what love is!"

Sterling rolled his eyes. "This is not the time for rom-com clichés! Decide!"

"I don't love either of them!" Adam shouted. "I only

love myself!"

Sterling pointed the gun at Adam, irritated. "That won't work, Adam. I won't shoot you. You can't outsmart me. Now, I told you if you didn't answer, I'd kill both of them. Is that what you want? Decide or I kill them both!"

"I can't."

"Don't miss your cue, Adam. Timing is everything!"

Adam pulled a quarter out of his pocket.

"Decide!" Sterling commanded.

Adam flipped the coin and read it off the back of his hand. "Rachel!" he said.

"No!" Sterling was incensed. "No props! No crutches! Who do you love most?"

"Polly! I love Polly most!"

"Are you sure?!"

"I'm sure! I love Polly the most."

On the TV, Alejandro Iñárritu was listing the nominees for Best Director. The camera was favoring Ridley Scott.

Sterling leveled his gun on Polly. "I thought as much. I'm sorry, Polly."

"Bullshit," Crush said. "You're not doing this for Christina. You're doing this because Adam stole your idea for an outer-space *Don Quixote.* Isn't that right?"

"Well, it was *my* idea! *My* conception! It would have put me back in the game, but this *hack*, this *drudge*, this *poser*, he stole it from me! Like he could ever have come up with something like that! It was my last chance!"

Alejandro was opening the envelope. "And the Oscar goes to...Adam Udell for *The Winter of Our Discontent.*"

The room fell silent. The audience in the Dolby Theatre applauded and a camera searched in vain for Adam.

"Fuck me," said Adam.

"Fuck," said Sterling. "*Fuck!*" He raised his gun to Polly's head. "It doesn't matter. Goodbye, Polly."

Sterling's finger flexed on the trigger.

Crush pushed aside his pain, summoned all his strength, and launched himself from the chair. He drove his bald head like a battering ram into Sterling's chest and brought him to the ground.

Just then Polly wrenched the arm of her chair free and brought it down on Sterling's head. Crush collapsed, clutching his gut and squeezing his eyes shut in agony. Then he heard it—the scuffling of feet and a click, click, click, like a dozen crickets chirping in unison.

He opened his eyes. He saw a half-dozen crazy-looking people pointing cameras, snapping pictures, and shouting at them to look this way. The paparazzi had arrived, riding to the rescue. Crush closed his eyes and drifted away.

CHAPTER TWENTY-TWO

Crush hated hospitals. He hated the beds. He hated the lime-green walls. He hated the food. He hated the doctors. He hated the nurses. He hated the pain. He hated the painkillers. He hated being tied to an IV bag. He hated having to drag the IV pole into the bathroom when he had to pee, even though he had an adjoining bathroom all to himself. He hated being awakened every hour for pills and punctures and the taking of blood pressure. Most of all he hated the monotony.

But even if he seemed surly and grumpy, he liked it when he had visitors. No matter who they were. He raised his right arm, the one that wasn't drilled with IV needles, and jangled the handcuffs that bound him to the bed.

"Are these really necessary? I'm not going anywhere."

"You jumped bail," Lieutenant Savoy said.

"I was going to come back."

"So you say."

"When are you going to learn to trust me, Savoy?" Crush said. He was feeling a little lightheaded from the painkillers. He resisted the temptation to ask the lieutenant out on a date. It didn't seem like the right time. Maybe later, after the trial.

"I'll trust you when you start telling me the truth," she said.

"I've been telling you the truth."

"The whole truth."

"You don't have time for that."

"What happened in the house on Mulholland Drive?"

"I thought you wanted to know what happened in the cemetery in New Orleans. Make up your mind."

"I don't think I can know one without the other."

Crush smiled weakly. "I like you, Savoy. I wish we could have met..."

"Under different circumstances?"

"I was going to say in a nightclub, but that'll do."

She stepped closer to him. "I don't think you shot that guy in the cemetery."

"You don't?"

"No."

"That's nice to hear."

"But you'll do time for it if nobody else turns up."

"That's not so nice."

"You want to tell me who really did it, Crush?"

Crush laid his head back on the rock-hard pillow and they talked around and around for another half an hour. In the end he buzzed the nurse for morphine and went to sleep.

In his dreams he was being interrogated by Lieutenant Savoy but he was naked and, after a while, so was she. Then the interrogation room turned into Adam's house and Savoy turned into Polly and the interrogation turned into lovemaking. He liked that better.

Unfortunately, he woke up before it got good. He looked across the room and saw a woman there. In his morphine-addled state, he thought it was Polly. Or hoped it was. Rachel walked into the light. "I'm glad you're not dead," she said.

"Yeah. If you hadn't had your Where They Are app going, I would be. I was never so happy to see paparazzi in my life."

"It's called wherearethey.com. The app updates every two hours and, to tell you the truth, I'd forgotten about it."

"Brandon didn't."

"No."

"He tried to save you. He gave his life for you."

"I guess he did."

"How's Adam?"

"He's good. He's very happy about the Oscar."

"Are you going to get me out of here?" Crush lifted his arm to show off the handcuffs. "I'm still under arrest, you'll notice."

"He can't confess."

"Of course he can't."

"He's on top of the game now. You can't expect him to give all that up."

"And the little matter of Kristin Quinn?"

She rolled her eyes. "Nobody's going to believe Sterling about that. Not after what he did."

"Are you staying with Adam?"

"Yes. I love him."

"You left him before. You went to stay with ten Berge."

"That was because I was afraid. I've never felt this way before. I thought that once I got Adam's stuff it would be over. Like it usually is. I tried to leave. I couldn't. This is for real, Crush."

"That's very touching. I hope this marriage turns out better than your last one."

"My last one?"

"To Brandon Renbourn. I thought he was demented

when he said he married you. But I was wrong, wasn't I? You did marry him. Under the name Eve Sidwich."

Rachel smiled. "You figured that out, huh?"

"Yeah, I thought that name sounded familiar," Crush said. "I Googled it. It's Barbara Stanwyck's character in *The Lady Eve*. She plays a con woman in that one."

"I thought it was appropriate."

"Brandon was your tool. You had him threaten you. Made Adam feel protective toward you. You even had him wait for you in the cemetery. But how did you get Bub there? Did you turn him? Get him to help you by offering a cut of Adam's fortune? Or did you offer him something more...tangible?"

"That's not a very nice thing to say, Crush."

"I'm not feeling very nice."

"I offered him money. Money is what most people want."

"I've noticed that."

"Shall I tell you the plan? And how it went wrong?"

"Sure."

"We were supposed to come out of the mausoleum and find you unconscious. Bub was supposed to come out of the shadows and Adam was supposed to shoot him. In the chest. A Kevlar vest would protect him. Then my dad was supposed to show up and tell Adam that Bub was dead. We were to hide 'the body' in the tomb. Adam would be bonded to me then. By the secret."

"Do you really have to pretend to kill a man to get Adam to marry you?"

"You have no idea how hard it is to get someone in show business to commit." She shook her head. "But it all went wrong. Adam shot him in the head. Killed him. What are the odds of that? And Dad didn't show up. So I had to improvise."

"By framing me?"

"That was Adam's idea, I swear. He put the gun in your hand and pulled the trigger. Then we hid the body. We didn't think anyone would find it. But Brandon...he went to the police and told them where 'you' hid the body. He was jealous of you. Isn't that silly?"

"It's hilarious."

"But I knew you could handle it. I knew you're a clever man and you'd find a way out of it. And I knew you'd want to protect me. Like you did when we were kids. I'm so sorry."

Crush looked at her for a long moment. "You know, I've figured out why you're such a good liar. You *believe* your lies when you tell them. You're a *method* con artist."

"I suppose I deserve that. But all the good things about me, my love for my father, my love for you, my love for Adam—they're *real.* Doesn't that count for something?"

"I suppose." Crush swallowed hard. Then he called out, "Did you hear that, Lieutenant Savoy?"

Savoy stepped out from the bathroom holding her cell phone. "I did. I got it on tape, too."

Rachel didn't blink more than once. She was back in survival mode. "That will never hold up in court."

"We'll see," Savoy said. "You're under arrest."

Rachel grabbed the IV pole, knocked it over in front of Savoy and made a run for it. The IV needles yanked themselves from Crush's arm. He spurted blood all over the sheets. Savoy untangled herself from the IV tubes while a nurse ran in to see what was the matter.

"What the heck are you doing in here?" the nurse asked.

Savoy was on her cell phone calling for backup to

cover the doors and stop a fleeing woman. Then she ran out herself, calling over her shoulder that Rachel couldn't get far. Crush admired her confidence. He knew better.

They never caught her. Rachel was that good.

◉

Eleven months later, Crush was manning the door of the Nocturne, keeping his eye on the Wednesday-night crowd. His recovery had been slow. The bullet had done a lot of damage to his insides, and he'd been in the hospital for two months. The hospital stay alone had taken its toll on his muscle tone. The surgery had done the rest.

With Gail's help, he'd gradually regained his strength, though he was still far from his top form. When he'd first retaken his post at the club (now with a post-apocalypse-dystopian-future décor), a few of the tough regulars thought they could take advantage of his weakened state. Even at half strength, Crush could still stand his ground and throw them off the premises. It felt good to know he could still do that.

Crush rarely thought about Rachel and Adam and New Orleans. Rachel had never been apprehended. She was famous, and everybody knew her face. That made her disappearance all the more mysterious and newsworthy. The Manic Pixie Dream Girl was on the run.

Byron Douglas had turned state's evidence in the Christina Manheim/Kristin Quinn murder case. He led the authorities to where he and Adam and Lloyd had buried her body in the San Gabriel Mountains.

Adam Udell was arrested. While awaiting trial in his house on Blue Jay Way, he committed suicide by injecting himself with Propofol and drowning in his infinity pool. He still had the Oscar though. Nothing could take that away from him.

Polly had retreated back home to North Carolina. She'd never contacted Crush. He had tried not to take that personally. A lot of crap had fallen down around her.

Sterling Bolsinger died of a myocardial infarction in his apartment before he could be brought to trial for the murders of Lloyd Fury and Alva ten Berge. As he'd predicted, he had an epic obituary.

Crush still felt a little pain in his gut. Perhaps it was just that he imagined the foot or so of intestines the surgeons had to remove. Perhaps it was the memory of the impact of the bullet as it pierced his stomach. Whatever it was, it would pass, he told himself.

The night was getting long. Zerbe had sent him a text a few hours ago, his Marcus Aurelius quote for the day: "The best revenge is not to be like your enemy." Crush wondered if Sterling had ever read that one.

Gail was manning the bar as usual, and she gestured for Crush to come over. He made it through the mob of Mad Maxes and Furiosas to the massive bar and leaned over it so she could talk to him over the blaring of the Arctic Monkeys through the speakers.

"Someone wanted me to give you something," she said, sliding a large envelope across the bar.

He opened it and looked at Gail for an explanation. She pointed to a table in the corner. Crush made it to the table and pulled out a chair. "Hello, Polly," he said.

"Hello, Caleb."

He laid the Letters of Transit out on the table. "These are the real ones?"

She nodded. "I took them for insurance. I knew Adam would close the iron door on me one day. I wanted to have something to cushion the blow. I put a copy in their place. Then somebody stole the copy. The joke was on them, wasn't it?"

"It was." She looked more beautiful now than she had before. Living without Adam had been good for her. Crush cleared his throat. "So how does it go? 'Of all the gin joints, in all the towns, in all the world, you have to walk into mine?' "

She smiled. "Yes, well, I've wondered how you were doing. And...I need help. I need money. It's a tough world out there. I need to sell these. I thought you might know somebody."

"Meier Lustig?"

"For instance."

"You could have contacted him yourself."

"I'd feel safer going through you."

"I see. Sure, I can help you."

"Thank you, Caleb." She took a last sip from her old-fashioned. "Send the money to this address in Raleigh." She handed him a card and stood up to go.

"How much do you want?"

"Whatever you can get."

"Is that all?" he asked.

She hesitated. "Just...we'll always have New Orleans, won't we?" And she walked out. *She's a good film editor,* Crush thought. *She knows when to cut to black.*

THE END

ABOUT THE AUTHOR

Phoef Sutton is a *New York Times*–bestselling author whose work has won two Emmys, a Peabody, a Writers Guild Award, a GLAAD Award, and a Television Academy Honors Award. The first novel in the Crush series, titled *Crush*, was a *Kirkus* Best Mystery of 2015 and a *Los Angeles Times* "Summer Reading Page-Turner."

Sutton has been an executive producer of *Cheers*, a writer/producer for *Boston Legal*, *NewsRadio*, and *Terriers*, and the creator of several TV shows, including the cult favorite *Thanks*. He is also the co-author, with Janet Evanovich, of the *New York Times* bestseller *Wicked Charms* and the brand-new *Curious Minds*. His other novels include the romantic thriller *15 Minutes to Live*.

Learn more at www.phoefsutton.com.